T0085882

TOURING THE LAND
OF THE DEAD

Maki Kashimada

TOURING THE LAND OF THE DEAD
& NINENTY-NINE KISSES

Translated from the Japanese
by Haydn Trowell

Europa
editions

Europa Editions
1 Penn Plaza, Suite 6282
New York, N.Y. 10019
www.europaeditions.com
info@europaeditions.com

Original Japanese edition published by
KAWADE SHOBO SHINSHA Ltd. Publishers.
This English edition is published by arrangement with
KAWADE SHOBO SHINSHA Ltd. Publishers, Tokyo
c/o Tuttle-Mori Agency, Inc., Tokyo
First publication 2021 by Europa Editions

Maki Kashimada has asserted her right to be identified
as Author of this Work

Translation by Haydn Trowell
Original title: *Meido Meguri; 99 no seppun*
Translation copyright © 2021 by Europa Editions

The translation of this work was supported by an Australian Government
Research Training Program (RTP) Scholarship

Library of Congress Cataloging in Publication Data is available
ISBN 978-1-60945-651-1

Kashimada, Maki
Touring the Land of the Dead

Book design by Emanuele Ragnisco
www.mekkanografici.com

Cover illustration by Ginevra Rapisardi

Prepress by Grafica Punto Print – Rome

Printed and bound in Great Britain by Clays Ltd, Elcograf S.p.A.

CONTENTS

Touring the Land of the Dead

T he 10:00 A.M. Kodama service, Natsuko reminded herself.

There would be any number of shuttle buses once they got there, and there was still ample time before check-in. But even so, she wanted everything to go according to plan. She couldn't help but feel that if they were delayed for even just a few minutes, the whole trip would end up having been for nothing.

Taichi, however, was unaware of her thoughts. Having boarded the bullet train, his four bad limbs bumped against the seats here and there, until finally he came to the one designated on his ticket and sat down with a plump. If he were anyone else, his failure to show reserve with respect to his disability might, far from engendering sympathy, have invited nothing short of annoyed frowns. But he was oblivious to that kind of unreasonableness. He merely beckoned to her from his seat, as if his having found it by himself were some kind of great achievement.

Natsuko showed no wifely concern for her husband's difficulties. She had hovered all over him throughout his repeated hospitalizations, and the constant need to take care of him had left her emotionally exhausted. Now, as she walked behind him, taking the seat by his side, she looked at him coldly, perhaps even cruelly, as if she saw not her husband but a raw manifestation of unreasonableness itself. And yet Taichi, almost pitifully blind to the malice of others, and yet as innocently dependent on his wife as ever, turned his back to her, asking without words for her to remove his coat. Shortly after the train left the station, a cabin attendant began to move down the aisle with an in-car sales trolley. Before he could have a chance to pester her for one, Natsuko bought him an ice-cream. Taichi, in good spirits, immediately set to devouring it.

At long last, she was able to break free from her restraints, to tear off the pink cardigan that her mother had sent her.

It was to be a short trip, only two days. To anyone else, to anyone who hadn't gone through experiences like hers, that would be all it was.

It felt like the train had only just left the station, and yet it had already reached Shinagawa. After their marriage, Taichi had been struck by illness. Three years of repeated hospitalizations had passed since then, and five again since they had learned the name of the disease. Yet to Natsuko, as exacting as those eight years had been, they were still better than what had come before. She didn't want to call to mind the time before she had met her husband, and referred to her past only as *that life*. *That life*—truly, the only words with which she could describe those unspeakable experiences. Not poverty, not loneliness, not sickness, but *that life*.

But then, at the end of January, she had come across a notice on the bulletin board on the way to the supermarket.

Local Health Retreat. Special Accommodation Discount. 5,000 Yen Per Night. Weekdays Only Through February.

Reading it, she found herself being carried away, torn by a contradiction of callous pleasure and unbearable pain. It was the luxury resort hotel where she had gone with her parents and brother as a child.

Past Taichi's head, outside the window, each mountain that pierced the peaceful late winter scenery was, to Natsuko, a very real embodiment of the cacophony that disturbed the stillness of her heart. As though trying to run far away from it all, she slumped deep into the realm of recollection.

There was no doubt about it, that hotel—no, that health retreat—would have to be quite old by now.

"Ah, I'm finally home. My second home!" Natsuko remembered her mother crying out at check-in time, leaning forward on the leather sofa as if having an attack. She seemed to be appealing to someone—well, certainly to no one in particular—that the fact that no one quite believed her was so terribly unfair. The eight-year-old Natsuko drank her "welcome drink," an iced tea, in silence. Even her four-year-old brother, holding an inflatable rubber ring as he waited to go for a swim in the heated pool, must have realized that their mother was acting out of the ordinary, as he wore an expression of mute astonishment. And what about her father? Maybe he was going through the check-in procedures? In any event, her memories of him were weak. Her mother and the two children always tended to act as if he didn't exist. That everyone was indifferent to her father, always ignoring him, had seemed to her to be a matter of course. So it didn't really matter what he was doing.

Her mother kept going on and on about how wonderful the hotel was. She had been repeating the same story since before they had left home. Natsuko, fed up, wasn't paying her much attention. The crimson carpet was so vibrant that she found it stifling. The hotel had been there since her mother was a child, and even then, it must have been a long-standing establishment. Natsuko had been shown it countless times on the old monochrome 8 mm film and so felt as if she already knew more than she cared to about it. Her grandfather dressed in a tuxedo, like some silver-screen star. Her grandmother wearing a décolleté, extraordinary for the time. They were dancing in the salon, their movements looking so peculiar in the halting projection of the 8 mm film. She knew just how much her mother cherished that film. Everyone wanted to stay at that hotel at least once in their lifetime. That was what her grandfather would say. And her mother would often repeat those words to the young Natsuko, quite as if she herself had thought of them.

There had to be some reason why the once haughty seaside hotel had been reduced to a cheap health retreat. Natsuko had been a student when it was first opened to the general public, and every now and then would think about going there on a whim. It should have been so easy. Yet such thoughts had seemed to her to be divorced from reality, and in the end, she never did go back.

She had learned several things from the experiences that had visited her in *that life*. She felt as if she had seen the unseeable, but her memories were vague and cloudy, and she couldn't quite put them into words. Once, when she had been a child, there had been a news scandal about a debt-ridden household that went on a trip to Disneyland the day before their family suicide. Though still young at the time, Natsuko felt a strange attraction to the incident.

When, without her mother knowing, she took the magazine to her room, she discovered that the young girl had been the same age as her. She imagined again and again how the girl must have felt. Whether it would be fun to go to Disneyland the day before she died.

But Natsuko, having now passed through *that life*, knew. It would be.

She decided to go to the hotel at the end of February, when tourists would be fewest in number. Until then, she imposed on herself a lifestyle of abstinence and cleanliness. It wasn't as if she wanted for anything, but in her spirit of thrift, she polished the tableware until it sparkled, like a bird that maintains a tidy nest before taking off in flight. She was at peace, yet she felt as if her heart were overflowing with an unquenchable need to cry, consumed with a single thought—that she had nothing left to regret.

And so she told Taichi that they would be going on their first trip in eight years.

His response was just as she had expected. He glanced in her direction, and merely nodded, before returning his gaze to the TV. But so long as he didn't oppose her, she didn't really care how he reacted. He would never understand the significance of the trip. In any event, since the health retreat was being offered at a discount, they could go at an unprecedented price, so they wouldn't have to worry about the money, she told him. But who was she trying to convince? All he did, as if he hadn't been listening to her at all, was ask: "What's for dinner?" The question wasn't to mean that he regarded her as little more than a kitchen maid, and it wasn't as if they had reached a period of ennui in their marriage. It was simply that he had no idea how to please a woman, or a wife.

She withdrew a hundred thousand yen for the trip. She went to the ward office by herself, booked their stay at the health retreat by herself, and bought the tickets for the bullet train by herself. All the preparations she did by herself.

When finally she returned home, everything as ready as it could be, she found Taichi watching TV, as usual. It was some kind of show about an unbelievably wealthy man. But she too was carrying in her wallet ten notes of ten thousand yen apiece. She held back her obscure sense of excitement and looked to the screen. The man owned a hotel in Monaco and so could go there whenever he felt like it, and for free at that. But then there she was too— she who had made the daring decision to withdraw a hundred thousand yen. Immersed in that curious feeling of elation, her mobile began to ring. She looked at the number. It was her mother. She left it alone for a moment, merely staring at the display. She was caught by a vague premonition that if she were to answer, the whole trip might evaporate before her very eyes. "Aren't you going to pick it up?" Taichi asked. Unable to explain her reluctance, she finally pressed the answer button.

Hey, what are you doing? I'm laid up in bed, as usual. Has anything interesting happened? her mother began fawningly. Put simply, she had nothing to do. Surely she could have found something to occupy her time? Housework, a hobby, anything? But her mother's inability to find anything to do was like a chronic illness, and quite beyond helping. *By the way, did you get my cardigan? It's mohair, my favorite, pink, fluffy, with ribbons, and pearls on the knots of the ribbons. I was really taken by it.*

I'm watching TV, Natsuko said, trying to hang up. *What*

are you watching? Her mother wasn't about to let her go. For her, finding some way to distract herself from her endless boredom was surely a matter of great importance, a matter, even, of life and death. *It's a show about rich people from all over the world,* Natsuko answered. *They're talking about a man who can go to Monaco for free, whenever he wants.*

What? her mother spat out, before falling silent. From her tone of voice, Natsuko could tell that she was going to use her as an outlet for her anger. *I want to go to Monaco! Why is he allowed to go whenever he wants? And for free!*

I'm sorry, Natsuko apologized reflexively. She shouldn't have mentioned it. All she could do was apologize. *I don't know how, how much money he has, how he's able to do it . . . I don't know.*

Oh? I see.

Her mother went on and on about how her free time was driving her crazy, before finally hanging up. She surely saw herself as the victim. She, who couldn't go to Monaco for free whenever she wanted, was the victim. Natsuko knew that much.

As she retraced her memories, she heard Taichi call out—"No more ice-cream!"—and was pulled back to the present.

Glancing across at him, she saw that he had carefully taken off his protective cap, probably because the train carriage was so warm inside. His hair was sticking out in every possible direction.

"I was finally able to give it a good wash yesterday."

"Thank goodness it's healed."

Taichi narrowed his eyes, as if ruminating over some pleasant feeling. It was a pitiful expression, the expression of a man who believed that there was no such thing as maliciousness in the world, that even if it did exist out there somewhere, it could be consigned to the past and quickly forgotten. Natsuko could only offer a bitter smile at that way of thinking.

"There was so much dandruff, I had to wash it three whole times."

Taichi didn't understand much about himself. He probably didn't even properly understand just what his wife thought about him. And no doubt he had no interest at all in whether or not he was loved by others, respected, or made a fuss over.

Around ten days ago, unable to control his movements, he had fallen over and struck his head. The injury had required four stitches, so he hadn't been able to wash it. Natsuko had been planning to take him to a hot spring. To her, that was her sole way of atoning. So she had felt a rush of fear at the thought that she wouldn't be able to do that for him. One's torment is greater when they can't atone for their sins, she thought. But he made it in time. At the doctor's surgery, watching first one thread being cut from her husband's head, then the next, she felt a thrill that she hadn't experienced even in the throes of sex. When the stitches were all removed, Taichi looked around restlessly, scratching his dandruff-coated head.

Though he was but thirty-six-years old, his hair had already turned white from the repeated attacks. They came without any warning. One morning, a cry like that of a beast erupted from somewhere deep inside him, his body going rigid, his eyes rolling back in his head, foam building up around his mouth as he lost consciousness. For a few seconds, they were visited by a profoundly sacred silence, and Natsuko could hear only the sound of birds chirping. It felt as if another person had usurped her husband's body, and was saying to her: "No matter what kind of man you're with, you'll never be happy. You understand that now, don't you?" But it was just a cerebral attack.

Natsuko had felt a sense of déjà vu when the first attack struck eight years ago, as if she had already witnessed that very scene somewhere once before. But the attack that seemed to lurk at the corners of her memory was more abstract, more ideal. And she had been repeatedly tormented by the experience ever since.

When the seizures came, as they inevitably did, whatever it was that repeatedly took over Taichi's body would say to her: "You will never be happy." And then, without waiting for a response, it would disappear back where it had come. But she managed to get used to it. She wasn't worthy of finding happiness. That was what she felt, day after day, while she listlessly carried out her household chores, or played with the children at her part-time job at the children's center. Like a wound healing—naturally, slowly.

She felt a strange dryness on her lips. Right, she remembered, she had put on some makeup before leaving home this morning. She hardly ever wore makeup. She must have looked just like her mother, back when they had all gone to the hotel together as a family. Her mother—she had been wearing a new eye shadow from Yves Saint Laurent that had been all the rage at the time. A former airline stewardess, she took pride in her skill at applying makeup. "You're going to be a stewardess too, right?" Ever since Natsuko was little, her mother would always ask her that question, as if there could be no room for doubt. But Natsuko's reaction never satisfied her. *Lots of women long to become stewardesses, but only a chosen few are able to do it. You have to be beautiful, and tall, and mustn't wear glasses. It's all very exciting, travelling through the sky, going to foreign countries. And you might even get the chance to marry a pilot.* When Natsuko responded that she didn't see what was so exciting about all that, her mother would stare at her with pity in her eyes, and fall silent. But she would soon bring the subject up again. After all, being a stewardess was every girl's dream. She acted as if she believed, since she had given birth to a healthy daughter, that that daughter too should yearn to become a stewardess. But Natsuko was interested in simpler, manual labor, even if it didn't end up being exciting, even if it meant that she wasn't one of the chosen few. Between her mother and herself, she still didn't know who was the more run-of-the-mill. She had no idea at all.

And yet, even now, her mother would still try to associate her daughter, a part-time working housewife, with her idea of an airline stewardess. *That old woman next door told me she saw a real beauty passing by down the street.* Excited by this trivial incident, her mother had rushed to call her. *It must have been you, don't you think? Because you're my daughter.*

Her mother's endless stupidity never failed to exhaust her. Her neighbor had simply happened to see a beautiful passerby. But armed with no more information than that, Natsuko's mother believed that it must have been her own daughter. She believed that a beautiful passerby *ought* to have been her own daughter. What she really wanted was to be told was that she, a former stewardess, was beautiful. But unable to understand even that much for herself, she had called to say that it was Natsuko who was being praised. She didn't even understand what she herself was thinking.

Just before they had left, while Natsuko was doing her makeup, Taichi had been absorbed in a gravure magazine. He had bought an unfathomable number of adult DVDs and gravure magazines at a bargain price, and left them all strewn about the room. Like a collection of chocolates, or stamps, or stickers. Natsuko couldn't help but feel somewhat amused by her husband. He had the body of a man, and was interested in those of women—and that alone allowed him to hold onto his sense of masculinity. When she looked at it that way, she felt a smile forming on her lips. It would be a lie to say that she didn't harbor some degree of contempt toward him, but there was no denying that there was nonetheless something charming about it all.

Beyond the tunnel, the blue ocean burst out before them.

When they arrived at the station, Taichi proceeded headlong step by step with the help of his cane. Natsuko gripped his hand, wide and thick and covered with sweat. Whenever she held onto it, she felt as if he was the only person who truly cared whether she lived or died. So if she were to live, she decided, she would live for him. It wasn't as if she felt that there was anything particularly special about living for someone else's sake, but if it were for anyone else's sake but his, there would be no need for her to exist.

They passed through the ticket gate and reached the bus terminal. The stop for the shuttle bus had to be around here somewhere. When Natsuko spread open the map that she had picked up at the ward office, Taichi poked his nose over her shoulder to take a look, like an animal sniffing for food. But he couldn't have understood anything. The stop for the shuttle bus seemed to be the one furthest from the station. She brought her husband through the plaza, when she saw a foot bath. He would no doubt like to try it, she thought, but they didn't have enough time.

At that moment, he gave her hand a sudden tug.

"What is it?" she asked.

He pointed to a child at a pedestrian crossing. "You can't ignore the signal, not when there are kids around. They might copy you."

"I suppose you're right." Natsuko sighed, relaxing. Taichi could be persuasive, every now and then.

"Ah, what I wouldn't do for a *kaisendon*," he said, pointing, as innocently as ever, to a banner outside a nearby eatery.

Without uttering so much as a word, Natsuko led him into the restaurant. She had resigned herself to doing as he said. His stubbornness could be its own form of persuasion.

It was a set-meal restaurant, serving all kinds of local fish. Even though it was a weekday, the place was crowded with tourists.

Taichi's eyes shone as he read the menu. It was a bit expensive, Natsuko thought, but her husband didn't seem to have realized just how much she was stretching their finances. Natsuko ordered a *kaisendon*, and Taichi a *tekkadon*.

Their orders didn't come for the longest time. Silence fell over the two of them, but there was nothing unusual about that. They had never been a particularly talkative couple. But Natsuko, as a wife, had never felt dissatisfied by her husband's quiet disposition. She understood, at some vague level, that his life was fulfilled. And if he himself felt that it was fulfilled, there was no reason to deny him that. Even if his body continued to decline, and their finances too. And in order to complete that sense of fulfilment, it seemed necessary that she not say anything. Watching him sit there in silence, his eyes closed, she couldn't help but think of a wild animal soaking in a medicinal bath to cure its wounds. For her part, she didn't have anything in particular that she wanted to bring up either. If she were to start talking, she would no doubt end up telling him everything there was to hear about *that life*. But fortunately, her constant fatigue always invited her into a calm silence. She was simply too tired to tell him anything. Before she knew it, she wasn't even able to bring herself to cry. Not talking, not crying, but at least it wasn't boring. What kind of life was this, this state of nothing but denial?—but she put a stop to such thoughts, for they would surely just make her even more tired.

At long last, the two rice bowls arrived. Natsuko watched as her husband, his eyes closed, slowly lifted the slices of tuna into his mouth. He chewed slowly, no doubt due to his neurological disorder, and so looked as if he were truly relishing them. Natsuko remembered when she had gone once to a luxury Italian restaurant with her mother and brother. Back then, she hadn't yet married Taichi, her mother was living off a widow's pension, and her brother, though he had just graduated from university and found a job, hadn't stuck to it, and spent his days wallowing in idleness. All three of them had no sense of thrift, no sense at all of the value of money. Red sea bream carpaccio paid for by credit card at a luxury Italian restaurant. It wasn't real, she thought. That cold carpaccio, studded with green dill and caviar like miniature diamonds, didn't look like a fish that had been alive. She couldn't pin down its taste.

"This is hardly a high-class restaurant. That carpaccio was awful," her brother began to complain in his usual high-minded way. "And this is hardly a real chef's work. Looks more like some housewife put it all together."

"Oh, you say such clever things!" their mother laughed ecstatically, no doubt seeing in her son the figure of a connoisseur.

The restaurant should have been sufficiently high-class for the both of them, and the food wasn't at all bad. They certainly couldn't have known any more highly ranked or expensive places than that one. But by insulting that high-class restaurant, they wanted to make out that they were regular patrons of even higher-class ones. Who were they trying to fool? Themselves, of course. They would tell themselves that they were high-class people who frequented high-class restaurants. They were no more than con artists conning themselves. The two of them continued to talk, about restaurants run by famous chefs, about members-only bars. Her brother had an endless list of phone numbers belonging to such places on his mobile. He showed one of them to their mother. And after looking at the number, the two of them smiled in satisfaction, leaning back in their chairs with full stomachs. If they were to behave in such a way in front of anyone else, anyone outside of their family, they would surely be met with contempt—but of course, they had no experience of that. It had been a long time since they belonged to society. Now, they went through their lives without friends, or even acquaintances. And so, in their own world, according to their own values, they had concluded that they were special.

Natsuko couldn't eat any more and so gave her sashimi to Taichi. He, as ever, took it as a matter of course. He could eat anything, seemingly without end. Her mother and brother called him vulgar for that. They were always disparaging him.

Before finding her current position at the children's center, Natsuko had been working part-time at the ward office. The job involved hardly anything more than stapling together the bulletin for a group that the office ran for local children who weren't attending school. She wasn't an airline stewardess, but she was doing the kind of manual work that as a child she had always wanted, so she couldn't say that her wish hadn't come true. Once the bulletin was ready, she would be handed a bundle of papers to staple together. And the person who made that bulletin was Taichi.

Three months after they first met, Taichi told Natsuko that he had fallen in love with her at first sight, and asked her to marry him. There was no helping it—she brought him home to meet her family.

She had told them in advance that he would be coming, of course, but her mother hadn't put out so much as a glass of water for him.

"So, you're Natsuko's boyfriend?" Her mother looked him over doubtfully. Her brother wouldn't even take a seat, looming over the sitting Taichi with his arms crossed.

"Yes, that's right." Taichi smiled, and took a sip from a bottle of barley tea that he had brought with him.

"You said you work at the ward office?"

"Yes."

"The ward office." Her mother sighed.

Taichi began to introduce himself. That he was from a seaside town in Hokkaido, a wonderful place surrounded by nature—and that, in spite of that, he couldn't swim. On hearing this, Natsuko broke out into laughter, but the others remained stone-faced.

After a while, he ran out of safe stories to tell. Yet her mother and brother refused to bring up any topics of their own, and so the four of them sat in silence.

"Why don't we get something to eat? Won't you let me treat you all?" Taichi suggested, and for the first time both her mother and brother nodded in agreement.

"I'm not very familiar with the area though . . ." he added innocently, without understanding anything. Natsuko remained silent. Without uttering so much as a single word, her brother led them to a Korean restaurant.

"All that child ever wants is meat. Never mind that I'm in the mood for a nice *kaiseki* course," her mother muttered.

Her brother was the first to take a seat and, after looking at the menu, ordered a bottle of shōchū. Her mother sat down beside him, and he showed her the menu. "Why don't you get something to drink?"

"You know I can't hold it."

The two of them chatted lightly while thinking about what to order. Natsuko and Taichi weren't even given a choice. Her brother went ahead and ordered the deluxe *galbi* and the *samgyetang*.

Once the meat was all lined up on the table, her brother finally spoke up. "Well? Let's dig in. It isn't like we get to eat this kind of thing every day."

"But you're always eating *yakiniku*."

"Not this deluxe stuff. I'm not completely clueless when it comes to money, you know."

Neither her mother nor her brother said anything to Taichi. They wouldn't even glance in his direction. Taichi merely looked on while nibbling on a piece of *gyūtan*. Natsuko sipped at some cola, without even touching the food.

"Mom, try some of the *japchae*. *This* is the kind of thing that I'm always eating," her brother said elatedly.

The meal wouldn't end. Her brother just kept on drinking.

Finally, Taichi stood up. "I'm sorry, but I'm afraid I'll have to excuse myself. The last train will be leaving soon. Goodbye." He laid out several bills on the table apologetically before leaving. "It's been fun," he murmured in a low voice—but her mother ignored even that.

When they arrived home, her mother called a family meeting.

"Just how much does that man earn?" she asked sternly.

"I don't know."

"Impossible." She shook her head. "Thinking you'd marry a man without even knowing how much he earns. Show me the ring. Don't tell me he didn't even give you a ring?"

Natsuko took it off to show her.

"Such a small diamond. You poor thing."

"It's not the size that's the problem, it's the lack of taste," opined her brother as he gulped down a glass of water to soothe his throat, parched from too much liquor. "Just think how embarrassing it'll be when people find out it isn't a Harry Winston design."

Her mother nodded along in silence. Natsuko felt as if she were on trial.

"More importantly, which university did he go to? Has he ever spoken about politics or art?"

"A university in Sapporo, I think."

"I don't want a brother-in-law I can't discuss things with at *my* level."

Natsuko's mother had no doubt harbored these kinds of expectations for her daughter's future partner ever since her own husband had passed away. And her brother was no different. They would both cheat Taichi out of everything given the chance. Not just money. His pride as well. They would rob him of everything that he had. Because they were the kind of people who thought that they could take everything while giving nothing back. They had no reason to think that way, but that didn't stop them. For her mother, men were no more than objects for exploitation. She thought that she could have that kind of attitude toward them simply by virtue of being a woman. Ever since Natsuko was a child, she would often say to her: *Are you listening? When you grow up and find a boyfriend, he'll surely take you to a French restaurant, a beautiful place like a castle. And when the food arrives, he'll wait for you to start eating first. He'll just sit there, watching you for a while, before he starts eating. He'll tell you how cute you are. That's what they do. Men take a woman out to a restaurant, watch her eat, and then pay for it all themselves. That's romance. You'll love it.*

You'll love it. That's what her mother had said. Natsuko had no idea what *it* was. In any event, she wanted to marry Taichi. No doubt he was far removed from her mother's image of the ideal man. She had opened a hole in the shell that was her family and could feel the wind creeping in from outside. Vague though this feeling was, she knew that it was what she had been looking for. In all the years that she had been living with her family, this was the first time that she had felt a real sense of self.

During lunchbreak the following day, Natsuko and Taichi met in the cafeteria at the ward office.

"Your brother had a lot to drink yesterday, didn't he? Is he okay?" Taichi asked worriedly.

"He did, didn't he?" was all Natsuko said in response.

"Your mother didn't say much. Is she shy in front of strangers? Or did I do something wrong?"

"No," Natsuko replied sharply. "Not at all. My family is a bit weird. So it's okay if you don't want to marry me."

"Huh?" The pork cutlet that Taichi had been holding in his chopsticks fell to the floor with a silent thud. "But you're the one I'd be marrying, Natchan. What a strange thing to say! You were so nervous yesterday. You must be exhausted. Let's put it behind us. Just try to imagine the wedding. You'll be so beautiful!"

"I'm sorry." She should have thanked him, but for some reason, she merely hung her head in apology.

They got married as planned. As if Taichi hadn't realized anything about her family, not even the thinly veiled sense of disgust that they felt toward him. Nothing at all. Surely he must have felt some kind of discomfort? But she doubted that he would ever pinpoint its true identity.

Taichi finished his wife's leftover *kaisendon*. Natsuko looked once again at her watch. They could still make their schedule, maybe. "The bus will be leaving soon," she urged him, and the two of them left the restaurant.

Shortly before they reached the bus terminal, his cane

perhaps having gotten caught in the stone pavement, Taichi stumbled and fell to the ground. Natsuko picked up the cane, but merely stared down at her husband, while five or six passersby quickly surrounded him and helped him to his feet. He thanked them all with an embarrassed grin.

When they finally boarded the empty shuttlebus, Taichi waved to the small crowd that had come to his aid. "Such kind people," he said softly.

What about her family then? What did he think about her mother and brother, whom Natsuko couldn't call kind even out of hollow flattery? Maybe it was because they had gone on a trip, or maybe it was because she had finally been able to put some distance between themselves and her family, but she suddenly found that she wanted to talk to her husband about things that they had never discussed before.

She vividly remembered the day when her mother had been forced to let go of her apartment to pay off her brother's debts. That had been long after Taichi was no longer able to work. He and Natsuko lived in a small apartment, paying the rent out of his pension and the income from her part-time job. Her mother called her out of the blue, using her as an outlet for her explosive anger, as a scapegoat, as a means of avenging herself. *It's all your husband's fault!* her mother shrieked when she and Taichi went to visit. *This would never have happened if not for that worthless husband of yours!* She must have truly believed that, that if her daughter had married someone wealthy, he would have built her a new house. Taichi knelt formally on the living-room floor, hanging his head in silence. Why didn't he say anything? People liked Taichi, especially ever since he had been struck by his disability. No matter where he happened to fall over, people came to help him. Once, he had even been brought home in a police car. *He's brazen, completely shameless,* her brother had said hatefully. More than anyone, Taichi was unreasonably hated by others, but he was also unreasonably loved. There was no doubt that unreasonableness affected everyone in life, to one extent or another, but how was it possible to face that much of it and still be so indifferent to it all?

The bus began to climb the steep mountain slope. After passing some cheap inns and a bunch of hotels, the coast came into view down below. It was around here, Natsuko remembered, but the bus showed no sign of stopping. Every time it swayed left and right, the couple too swayed from side to side. Finally, they reached a point at the top of the mountain where there wasn't anything to see at all, and went through a narrow one-way tunnel before at last arriving at the hotel.

As soon as they stepped off the bus, she noticed that the rose garden by the side of the hotel had closed. The pink paradise that her mother, with her girlish tastes, had loved so much was now overrun with dead grass and closed to visitors.

"Ah," Taichi exclaimed. "The air's so fresh here. And the greenery . . ." He looked around casually, as if free from all worry.

The hotel had seen better days. The frame around the automatic door at the entrance was rusted over. The glass was a pale blue in color. The eight-year-old Natsuko hadn't felt anything at all when she had gazed through that pale blue glass, but looking at it now, she could feel the weight of that old, neglected automatic door. Maybe it was because of the time of year, but the once bustling lobby stood empty. Only the old grand piano remained as she remembered it.

When she finished checking in at the front desk, she noticed that Taichi had sat himself down in a wheelchair. The hotel staff must have prepared it for him. He sank into the backrest with content, without showing any sign of embarrassment or humility. Truly, he was like little more than a piece of luggage. She doubted that he would even mind being treated that way. She pushed the wheelchair slowly as the staff guided them both to a sofa by the window. Taichi said nothing by way of thanks.

The couple sat down, and a beautiful woman with long, slender legs, her complexion unusually dark for a Japanese, brought them some pineapple juice. It was a welcome drink, she said. In the past, they would also have been offered tea or coffee, hot or iced, whatever they wanted—but no longer. No sooner had Taichi taken the cup than he had gulped it all the way down.

Natsuko stared at the carpet. Only that carpet was unchanged. That red feeling of oppression was just as she remembered it.

Okay, choose whatever drink you like, she remembered her mother saying when she was eight years old. Quite as if she herself were offering it to Natsuko. *At this hotel, you can have whatever you want, for free, as much as you like.* Of course, no one would want to drink that much tea or juice, but her mother was probably just happy that it was being offered to her.

For free, as much as you like. That was what that wealthy man, the one who could go to Monaco whenever he wanted, had said. For her mother, back then, being treated that way must have felt like a matter of course. *For free, as much as you like.* Tall waiters dressed in white shirts and black bowties, carrying more glasses than anyone could possibly drink on their silver trays. Her mother's high heels sinking into the crimson carpet. *We should go for a swim in the heated pool before evening. Oh, but it might be even nicer after dinner. At night, they light up the pool, you know.* A group of men wearing well-starched shirts, each holding a cigar idly in one hand, stood chatting in a group. They seemed to be acquainted with the hotel manager. No doubt they were the kind of exclusive members who squandered their money at the hotel, staying in its most luxurious rooms whenever they visited. They kept on chatting, their welcome drinks standing untouched on the table. Her mother must have felt as if she too had become a member. She was quite capable of deceiving herself. Because she was completely incapable of looking at herself from the outside.

Back when I was little, when I came here with your grandfather, we had a whole suite to ourselves. He was a member, you see. It was wonderful, more wonderful than you could ever imagine. That day, her mother had been at her most talkative.

Her grandfather had undoubtedly relished his summer vacations. He had loved hot summers. *So long as it's warm, I don't care where I die,* he had said. He wouldn't have even minded being killed on the battlefield, so long as it was somewhere in the South Seas. But he had been struck by malaria during the war and so returned home alive, ultimately founding a small business through which he built his fortune. Her mother must truly have been proud of such a dependable father. In his later years, he came down with emphysema and died sooner than anyone could have foreseen. By then, he had become so invisible that not even flies bothered to take note of him. And so he had disappeared, fading away into nothingness, without leaving her mother anything in the way of an inheritance.

The staff were describing the hotel's various dining options. They handed her a pamphlet. Looking at it, Natsuko saw that there was a salon on the fifteenth floor. It was that salon. The 8 mm film started playing in her head. Her mother as a child, the hem of her skirt flowing wide as she spun around and around playfully.

Their room was on the seventh floor. There were two old but clean and tidy beds. There was no comparison to the beds in the suite room where her mother had jumped about so friskily in the 8 mm film. Taichi managed to lay himself down. *I love these Western-style beds,* he laughed. *They don't make my back hurt.* Natsuko went to take a look at the bathroom. As expected, the toilet was quite old, but there was no smell, and it was clean enough. The bath was narrow, but the hotel had a large public one that they could use, so that didn't matter.

In any event, the place had been reduced to a cheap, five-thousand-yen-per-night health retreat.

It was quiet. She thought that she saw something move in the corner of her vision. She turned around to see Taichi flopped forward on the bed, still wearing his coat, unable to get up. He mustn't have been used to keeping his balance while sitting on a bed. He didn't like wearing a belt, so his trousers and underwear had drooped down, and she could see the gap between his buttocks. She lifted him up and took off his coat.

As she approached the window, the cold sea spread out before her eyes. It was quiet, and she had no difficulty making out the sound of the waves breaking against the shore. There were some pigeon droppings stuck to the window, but she didn't care. It was only a five-thousand-yen room.

"I want to go to the salon," she said, and Taichi nodded to her in silence.

She sat him in the wheelchair, and they took the elevator to the fifteenth floor.

The salon was empty. There was absolutely nothing in the center of the hall. At the back was a stage, with a percussion setup and a keyboard. The floor was still waxed and polished, but it didn't look like it had been used in quite some time. How many high heels had once trodden on this floor? How many steps had been taken on it? Her grandmother wearing a dress, curtsying, and her tuxedo-clad grandfather taking her hand. Her mother's family, with their exclusive membership, had brought along a minder to look after the children—he was the one who had shot the 8 mm film, her mother had told her. Her young mother was wearing a wide-hemmed dress, with a ribbon tied around her chest, her face glowing with pride as she watched the dance. Then there was her mother's older brother dressed in short trousers, and her younger sister in an outfit that resembled a sailor-style school uniform. Her mother's brother, watching the dance from a leather sofa, was brazenly holding a champagne glass. And her mother herself, wanting to take a sip, was trying to snatch it away. There was something impenetrably startling about their actions, but in the middle of that monochrome world they flowed silently, matter-of-factly. *It's a special day today! It's finally summer!* Her grandfather had had that kind of personality and so had probably let the children drink whatever they wanted. And her mother had surely thought of that as an honor. Her young mother, thinking that she was special. Thinking that she was one of the chosen few. Natsuko was overcome with vertigo, her heart filled with disgust. Just as it was all beginning to become too unbearable, a round rubber ring cut across her vision.

The wheels reflected clearly on the floor. Truly inorganic wheels. Not high heels, but Taichi's—her husband's—wheelchair.

"There's nothing here," he said, looking up at her.

Right. There wasn't anything in the salon. Nothing at all. If there *was* anything there, it was only loss. The loss of her mother's childhood joy.

Let's take a dip in the hot spring, Taichi said innocently once Natsuko began to push the wheelchair. *I've been looking forward to the hot spring—the hot spring, and dinner too.* Maybe he had never experienced this kind of loss, the kind that never fully healed.

The wheels left long tracks on that cold floor, gleaming like the surface of a lake.

She pushed the wheelchair as far as the public bath on the first floor. *I don't feel like going in. I'll wait for you here,* she said, taking Taichi to the entrance of the men's bath. *The hotel staff will help me, so don't try to peek into the men's area, Natchan,* he said. Taichi had no questions, no concerns whatsoever about her, about her reluctance to go in. He was always like that.

The hotel staff supporting him, he proceeded into the men's area. Natsuko slumped down onto the sofa outside, her body going completely limp. Maybe it was because she had looked directly into someone else's past—into her mother's past. But the moment she was left alone, she was assailed by a sense of gratification quite at odds with her fatigue.

Taichi's awkward footsteps faded into the distance. She sat motionless, listening to them grow fainter and fainter. Finally, the sound disappeared altogether, and all she could hear was the crashing of waves. The crashing of the waves, which should have been like the steady flowing of a basso continuo, grew louder as Taichi moved away, the quietude stealing up on her. It moved at walking pace, but surely, confidently. She could even make out something else, the sound of wan strips fluttering out of sight. And then she finally realized what it was—the sound of countless dresses hanging in the darkness.

She stood up and approached the partitioning screen. There was a tremendous number of dresses behind it. According to the sign, guests could borrow them to dance in the salon. But there was no one there. No woman standing in front of the screen for a photograph, nothing reflected in the mirror. Just the dresses, dusty, giving off some unpleasant odor. Could the dress that her grandmother had worn in the 8 mm film have been borrowed from here? Only the dresses of the women in the monochrome film were filled with color. They began to waft with perfume, and the crystals attached to them began, one by one, firmly, coolly, to take back their radiance. The past, again, crept up on the present.

The memories washed over her. That florid scene of out-of-fashion dresses called to mind a cheap hostess bar. Her brother, freshly employed, was ecstatic at having gotten his hands on his first credit card. He had always loved hostess bars. *Let's have some fun in town,* he said, deciding just like that to take her out to a club.

The attack began late at night, after their mother had gone to sleep. "I'm so thirsty, I feel like I'm going to die," her brother said. "Why don't you buy a beer or something?" Natsuko asked. "I can't. I don't have any money. I'd have to use the card." There was no stopping him, once he got like this. He would climb into a taxi and set forth downtown. There was only one path open to her.

No matter how much you drink, it won't be enough. Maybe she should have said something like that.

Whenever they went out on the town at night, her brother would become obsessed with making her look pretty. Natsuko's dresser was filled with clothes that he had bought for her on his credit card. He would grab her by the hand and take her out to a department store, make her try on all kinds of clothes that he would pick out, and then buy them for her. After she got changed, he would sit her in front of a mirror, comb out her hair, and spray a luxury-brand perfume on her neck. Then he would say to her: *Natsuko, you* are *a woman, you know. If you would just make yourself look nice, everyone would pamper you. You might even find someone to take care of you and treat you special. But you don't even do that. All you have to do is brush your hair neatly, like this, just once a day,* he said as if trying to console her.

The two of them went into a dense alleyway lined with drinking houses, and were soon accosted by five or six hustlers. Natsuko felt ill at ease from the countless neon lights, her head spinning. After negotiating the price, one of the hustlers took them to the third or fourth floor of a mixed-residence building. It was the kind of place that one sometimes hears about where, if a fire were to break out and the emergency exits were blocked, countless hostesses and their clients would end up dying.

The two of them entered the club. Inside, there were women dressed in clothes of all different colors. Red, pink, purple, gold. The colors of the flames of women's fighting spirits. Dresses that showed off the secret intentions of men and women alike. When the two took a seat, the women came to sit next to them. But as soon as they began to be treated like customers, her brother's attitude toward her underwent a sudden change. He snatched away her bag, pulled out the envelope that contained her salary for the last month from her part-time job, and stuffed the notes into his own Italian-made wallet. All at once, he became suddenly loquacious. *Waiter!* he yelled, about to come out with some complaint or another. He always did that, no matter the situation. *It's too noisy in here,* he cried out in anger. Then, for some reason that she couldn't understand, he began to rail abuse at her in front of the hostesses.

"This woman, right, she's just so stupid. Like, really stupid. I'm not even kidding."

The two hostesses laughed. Professionals in dealing with even the worst of clients, they smiled calmly without any sign of surprise. They had no doubt come across a great many men who would start to behave strangely after a couple of drinks.

"And this woman, right, she's into other women. I'll bet you she's done it with one. You think she'd be willing to show her face here if she hadn't? Huh? That's what you're all thinking, right?"

Natsuko said nothing to contradict him. She merely drank her water in silence. She was so used to this kind of treatment that she felt neither anger nor agitation, only languor and drowsiness.

She suppressed a yawn.

"Don't! Don't you dare fall asleep! The night's only just started!" Her brother slapped her. She let him do as he pleased.

The hostesses feigned composure.

Well, I guess women don't normally come here, one of them said to her brother with perfect timing.

"Right? That's right, right? Why don't you tell her what kind of place women normally go to?"

That would be a host club, of course. That psychic on the TV, she makes a fortune. She's always going to host clubs, the hostess said, pointing to one of the overhead screens.

"Oh? That show there? So that's what she does with all that dough, huh?"

With the conversation shifting to TV personalities, her brother's interest finally turned to the hostesses. If not for that, there would have been no way of getting him to leave her alone.

When she got home, she fell asleep without even changing out of her clothes.

After two years, her brother eventually racked up an impossible debt on his credit card, and then went crying to their mother. "They won't leave me alone! I'm losing my mind!" Faced with no other options, their mother had to let go of her apartment to settle his accounts.

With his debts taken care of, her brother began to refer to that time as his "age of madness." He could give it some grand name, something like his "golden age"—he could call it whatever he liked, Natsuko thought, she didn't care. She was just so tired. He would talk like a French poet looking back on his days of abusing absinthe. But he was just a small-town alcoholic, and an unemployed one at that, someone who could afford nothing but the cheapest liquor.

Natsuko, unable to stay there even a moment longer, turned her back on the dresses hanging in the darkness. As if to flee from those reeking costumes, already completely faded.

For that matter, back then her mother had been incessantly going on about the film. "I want it colored. But the 8 mm makes the movements look weird, don't you think? I don't like it at all. Why can't it look more like it's happening right before my eyes? I'd watch it with my brother and his wife, and with my sister and her husband—we'd all watch it together. We'd have a screening at the hotel and reminisce on it all over a full course meal." Or she would start recounting its contents to her yet again. "I want to get the 8 mm film colored, that one from when we all stayed with your grandfather in the suite, the most expensive set of rooms in the hotel. Your grandmother was holding the camera. She introduced the huge living room first, then that huge bathtub, like something from overseas, and the toilet. Then there was a counter with a bunch of glasses all in a line, every single one of them completely spotless, and a mountain of fruit. And then it was us children, rushing up to that huge bed in the deepest room in the suite, right? We'd watch that film, watch ourselves jumping up and down on that huge bed, with my brother and sister, we'd all watch it, talking all about it." Had she been reminiscing about those past events in the hope that she could experience them all once more?

Natsuko watched as the sea drew ever nearer. There was a notice on the window: *Do not open*. There was no doubt about it: in the early afternoon light of summer, the sea would be an incredibly deep and beautiful shade of blue. But now, the sky was cold, and nothing but black waves and white foam stood out in the late winter evening. That was it: the white foam looked just like the foam that dripped from her husband's mouth whenever he had his attacks.

To Natsuko, Taichi's attacks were something that she could happily call convulsions in the fabric of life itself. The first one came quite as if it was aiming for that very moment. After all, even if he did work, her family would deprive him of everything that he earned, so it would be better for him not to work at all, she had thought.

The operation was a major one and involved embedding an electrode into his skull. At the time, he couldn't control the tremors in his limbs and tongue at all. The doctor told them that they could be treated by passing an electric current through his brain.

First, he explained the operation to them. It involved going under general anesthesia, so there were some patients who decided not to go through with it. No matter how good their luck, if she lost Taichi, she would be left with neither principle nor interest. She steeled herself against the worst.

They were shown a video. The patient's tremors weren't so strong as Taichi's, and he wasn't under general anesthesia. Still, it was a daring surgery. The patient's head was cut open, with his brain lying there exposed. Finally, the patient, with the electrode embedded in his brain, wrote the word "nerves." The trembling of the hand that until now had been uncontrollable was brought to heel, and the characters stood out vividly.

The surgery seemed to be quite dangerous, and so Natsuko would have liked to have had more time to think about it. But the doctor told them that someone else who had been scheduled to undergo the operation early the following week had suddenly cancelled, so they should decide as soon as possible if they wanted to secure the place. There was a long waiting list for the surgery, so if they put it off, they might have to wait over five years.

And so Taichi, his tongue trembling, said slowly: *I'll have the surgery. I'll have the surgery.*

Hey, they would be putting you under general anesthesia, and putting an electrode in your brain. Let's think about it a little more, Natsuko suggested. But Taichi said again: *I'll have . . . the surgery.* His body might have been weak, but his resolve was strong.

She could hear the sound of the waves breaking. It seemed to grow louder each time the water crashed against the shore. First, her wealthy grandfather passed away. Then, her father died from some mysterious brain disease. It had all started around that time, the weariness that struck at them all, until at last they found themselves living in poverty, and in the end, the heart of this creature that was her family began to whither. Little by little. Like the speed at which the waves were beating against the shore. If she could look at *that life* directly, surely she would be able to shed at least one tear? That way, maybe even she, who had completely given up on both family and future, would be able to cry. Even if she was the only one who actually believed it, didn't she want to think that she herself was worth crying over? Finally, those emotions grew louder even than cymbals, and at the moment she turned her ears away from it all, she heard a voice calling out her name. Out of the mist tottered her husband like a steamed bun. Regaining her footing in the present, she went to help him.

* * *

No sooner had Natsuko rushed her husband back to their room than the phone rang. It was dinnertime. They could choose among a Japanese-style meal, a Western-style meal, and a buffet. Taichi, without the slightest hesitation, chose the buffet.

When they entered the warmly lit dining hall, a waiter offered to push Taichi's wheelchair. It seemed that only the dining hall had been redecorated since Natsuko had come as a child. She felt, for some vague reason, a sense of relief. There was a ramp between the entrance and the main area, so the wheelchair posed no problem.

Holding on tightly to his cane, Taichi wandered over to the serving area without relying on anyone's help. Just as he always did. He liked to do everything for himself, and he would no doubt keep on doing so. There was a poster in the hall. The health retreat was holding a Hokkaido Fair. Perhaps Taichi, a Hokkaido native, wanted to try out food from his hometown at this tourist site. He certainly looked to be enjoying himself, shuffling back and forth with servings of Ishikari *nabe*, salmon carpaccio, and bowls of salmon roe over rice. He was, in a certain sense of the word, indifferent toward food.

The poster depicted a beautiful field of purple lavender spreading out all the way to the horizon. What kind of place was Hokkaido? Natsuko wondered. She had never been there. Her mother, who for no good reason regarded Taichi's rural family with contempt, had arranged both the traditional exchange of gifts and the wedding reception all by herself, and so Natsuko had never had an opportunity to have a proper conversation with Taichi's parents. And after he was struck by his disease, Hokkaido began to seem more and more distant. Terrifyingly distant. What was there to see or do? Some part of her wanted to find out.

"What's the matter? Aren't you hungry?" Taichi asked her worriedly.

She had taken some mozzarella from the counter, but hadn't so much as touched it. She could hear the sound of the waves. Her tears, the waves of her emotions, had taken the form of a deep, soughing basso continuo. There was a sea in her heart, always undulating. She looked at Taichi. There was a cut on his chin. He must have nicked it while shaving.

She sat lost in thought, staring at the immaculate table-cloth. That pure whiteness, unmarred by even a single drop of blood, spread out before her. The word *clean* seemed to fit. But it was unnatural, unhealthy even, that there wasn't so much as a single drop of blood to be seen. Not anywhere in that restaurant, nor the famous hotel, nor its top floor, not in that French restaurant, and not on the tablecloth either.

Even after she married Taichi, her brother would frequently call their apartment. *Something's come up. I need to see you. Now.* That was the kind of thing he would say.

She had lost count how many times. She could never resist him. *I've booked us a table at that French restaurant, on the top floor of that hotel. There's something important I need to tell you.* But this was just an excuse. All he really wanted was to go somewhere fancy to eat. He no doubt meant to put it on his credit card, or else had stolen some money from the drawer where their mother kept a ready supply of cash. *There's a dress code, so go and get changed first.* He sounded like he had only just learned the words. Natsuko dressed formally, as always, putting on red lipstick.

They met in the lobby, quite as if they were a couple coming for a date. Her brother strode around as if he owned the place. He would no doubt force her to drink something expensive with him.

He gulped down his glass of champagne. *Ah, this is the stuff,* he said. *There's nothing quite like expensive food. It really makes you feel like you're alive.* So he thought that this was living, did he? And then he would always start talking about the same thing. *Hey, so when are you going to divorce him? You don't get it, do you? You're only with him because you're lonely, you know? You don't really love him. Do you? He won't work, he won't do anything at home. How could anyone love that kind of guy?* But someone who couldn't do anything was still better off than a dead man, Natsuko thought. Her brother was simply jealous of Taichi's life. *How on earth could you love someone who won't do anything for us?*

And then, as if he had just invented the method himself, he said: *Look, this is how you eat it.* In front of him, on top of that white tablecloth, was a plate of tonguesole meunière. He handled the dish with a surprising level of dexterity. He was being awfully sociable. He called the waiter over. *There's some venison coming after this, right?* he asked. *The venison this time of year is the best.*

This is just basic etiquette, got it? he pointed out to her. *You don't have much common sense, so pay attention.*

The wine was beginning to kick in. He moved on to a topic that made her want to vomit in disgust.

I'm going to France, he said. *To study. At the Sorbonne.*

Before that, it had been Harvard. Whenever he started talking about studying abroad, Natsuko could only lower her head. Such conversations were, to her, a form of torture. First, he was going to study philosophy, then economics, then art. A cacophony of incoherent delusions. She stared at the knife on the tablecloth. She wanted to use that knife, to make a little cut somewhere that would make her blood come pouring out. How angry it would make her brother if she were to stain this white, unhealthy tablecloth with her blood. He would no doubt think that it was his immaculate pride that had been wounded. But she doubted that she would ever be able to go through with it. She wanted to go home, she wanted to go home and watch that TV show with that rock singer from Hokkaido that Taichi liked so much. She wanted to watch it with her husband and, more than that, to watch him, to return to the life that, though it never failed to exasperate her, still left her feeling somehow satisfied.

You poor thing, her mother would say. *You poor, poor thing. Working so hard in place of your husband at that drab job of yours. I feel so sorry for you.* Even though what was really deserving of pity were those hours spent in that restaurant looking at that tonguesole meunière, that evening spent together with someone who couldn't understand her at all, in that gorgeous world in which she didn't belong. It was all coming back to her again. Even her colleagues at the ward office acted that way. *It must be so hard for you,* one of them had said to her. *If it were me, I would get so exhausted, you know? But you keep on going, in silence, without complaining to anyone. Don't you ever get tired of it? Isn't it painful? It sounds like torture.* But her colleagues certainly had no idea what real torture was. What was painful, truly painful, was having to spend time with ghosts who wouldn't rest in peace, people who had yet to realize that they had long since given up on both hope and future.

That was why, for as long as she could remember, Natsuko's senses of hope and desire had already faded. She had never dreamed of becoming an idol, as normal girls did. Nor had she dreamed of becoming an airline stewardess, like her mother. Even when her mother brought it up, she had never seen herself heading toward some spectacular future. She had already given up on everything. And she never thought too deeply about why such unreasonableness, such unfairness, such unhappiness always befell her. She lived her life trying to think about it all as little as possible. Because it wasn't the kind of thing that you could easily look at, not directly. And if, by chance, she *were* to glance on it, she knew that it would leave an unhealthy, fatal wound, the kind from which not even blood would flow. Only her mother and brother immersed themselves in memories of a happy past, dreaming, and talking endlessly about their dreams. All Natsuko could do was block her ears. She was never able to tell them to be quiet. If she did, if she told them the truth, the little world in which they immersed themselves would no doubt collapse. And then her brother would say to her:

Give me a break, would you? They're the ones who're all messed up in the head. It's them. All they ever do is deny every single one of our possibilities. And based on what? And so she couldn't even bring herself to feel angry. If she were to get angry at them, she would just end up tiring herself out. Hers was simply a weary body, trying to preserve itself. She couldn't understand why it tried so hard to keep on going, why it had to keep on living. If it were to die, *that life* would end forever. The noise would come to a stop.

That was how she had felt when she first met Taichi. She couldn't pin down exactly why, but she found herself wanting to marry him. She could only imagine her mother's resentment were she to wed a man so far removed from her mother's ideals. Some evil influence practically tempted her to do it.

Before she introduced Taichi to her, her mother had said: *We'll have to go to Monaco for your honeymoon. I'd love to visit Monte Carlo.* She took it for granted that she would go with them. And her brother too, of course. They both loved to gamble. It was a way of making a fortune out of nothing, without spending any effort at all. They believed in that kind of magic. So Natsuko and Taichi ended up simply not having a honeymoon.

But the one who always met with good fortune was Taichi. Like when he was able to have the brain surgery so soon due to a sudden cancellation. The same people who wouldn't spare Natsuko a second glance would, for some reason, shower Taichi with all manner of kindness. It happened all the time. Even at the hospital. "I'm sorry about my husband. He can be so stubborn," she would say. But the doctor would merely laugh: "He sure is, isn't he?" And he would pat Taichi on the head. The doctors were only kind to Taichi. When they spoke to her, they did so coolly. "After all, a doctor is a patient's ally," her mother once said, flaring her nostrils with resentment as she all but spat out the words.

The hospital to which Taichi had been admitted was the same one that Natsuko's father had gone to. That was no coincidence. It had a specialist neurosurgery ward, and so other institutions would send their patients there once they had given up on helping them.

It must be some kind of horrible disease, her mother said. *He'd already started getting dementia. Yes, I'm sure of it. No matter how many years passed, you were always nine to your father. And you know, he would always find a way to sneak out, to withdraw some cash using a card on the verge of expiring, and then he'd use the money to go drinking. And I was the one who always caught the blame for it. Why did they have to do that?*

When her mother spoke like this, her face showed no sign of sadness. Only annoyance. As if, while facing her daughter, she wanted to say: *They should have blamed your father. They should have blamed him, not me. Why didn't they punish* him?

Without exception, her mother's stories always ended up descending into a litany of complaints. Even now, Natsuko could hear her rambling on: *Once, the doctor said to me that I wasn't coming to visit him enough. The hospital was so far away, but he didn't care. He told me that I should come more often. And then he asked me—me!—whether I had a lover somewhere, whether that was why I wasn't coming as often as he thought I should. I ran off to the bathroom, sobbing so hard! It's true! I couldn't stop sobbing.*

Her mother would go on telling this story for years after Natsuko's father passed away. Quite as if she were recounting it to her for the first time all over again. And it always ended the same way, with that word, *sobbing*. It never failed to get on Natsuko's nerves every time she heard it. She couldn't accept that word, *sobbing*, on a purely physical level. It drove her crazy. She always thought that the most miserable part of the story wasn't her father's idiotic behavior, nor the horrible way that the doctor had treated her mother, but rather that hopelessly stupid word, *sobbing*. That was how she felt. Her mother couldn't forgive her father, nor the doctor either. She wanted to convey how unfairly she had been treated, how miserable and unhappy it had all made her. But the only word that she had to express that tragedy, the only word that ever came to mind, was always that one—*sobbing*.

Whenever she heard it, Natsuko thought that no matter what kind of unhappiness were to befall her mother, she wouldn't change, that even if an altogether different kind of unhappiness were to befall her, she would still insist on using that word, *sobbing*. She had no other way of expressing herself. It was pitiful, really. She would finish off that episode the same way, *sobbing,* forever, without ever having learned anything from it. And what was even more miserable about it was that she herself wouldn't realize that fact at all. Even if it were pointed out to her, she wouldn't accept it, or else she would suffer a mental breakdown. She no doubt still thought that she could be treated like a princess. She believed that the age of her own father, that time when she had been given everything, for free, as much as she wanted, would no doubt return. And if that certainty were ever to be thrown into doubt, she would end up *sobbing* all over again.

And so, Natsuko thought, she would never be able to leave her mother. She would be stuck with her forever. She had no common sense, none at all, and was simply too incompetent to live by herself. Whenever something that she didn't like happened, she would end up *sobbing*, like a little girl, always waiting for someone else to come and fix it for her. And that someone would inevitably be Natsuko.

Her brother too thought of himself as unhappy. However, for him, it was that very sense of unhappiness that had convinced him that he was one of the *chosen few*, that he was destined to accomplish great deeds far beyond those of the average man.

For him, unhappiness was belonging to a family that had no money.

"If only we had more money," he would say. "If only Mom had the money to support me studying overseas, I'd be able to reach for greatness. All I need is the chance, and I'd be able to do practically anything." He always spoke like that when he got worked up. Though he couldn't see it, his real unhappiness stemmed from his insatiable yearning for a wonderful version of himself, for a wonderful world just out of reach. He thought it so unfair that these things didn't exist for him, and had convinced himself that he was the victim of some great injustice.

He didn't understand. That those things that he ruminated over vaguely—a wonderful version of himself, a wonderful world—existed only in his imagination. Certainly, there was probably an element of truth to the saying that life is made up of waves. If you are beset on by unhappiness, it isn't unreasonable to expect happiness to have its turn in the future. However, those waves would not come in any way that would satisfy him. The happiness of the high tide wouldn't bring the wonderful little world that he was waiting for.

For him, who yearned for things that didn't exist, he was in the right, and it was nothing short of injustice that he couldn't have them.

Sometimes, when he drank himself into a stupor, he would start to cry. "I just wanted to work for people. All I ever wanted was to be useful to someone." He really believed that. He really did want to do something for someone else—so much so that he would be happy even to be their slave.

"Ah, I'm stuffed. I wonder if I can fit any more in . . ."

Natsuko glanced up at the sound of Taichi's voice, only to see that he had surrounded himself with a long row Yūbari melon jellies. *These jellies are really famous, you know—everyone in Hokkaido eats them.* That incredibly warm, ripe orange color had been a good friend to him ever since his childhood.

When they went back to their room on the seventh floor, Taichi, as usual, switched on the TV. He never missed this program, and so while they might not have been in their usual surroundings, it felt almost as if they were still at home.

"Say," Natsuko began, her eyes directed at the screen. "This hotel . . . I've been here before."

"Oh?"

"And my grandfather too. He brought my mother here when she was little."

"Huh? It's that old, is it?"

The comedian on the TV was playing the fool. A wave of laughter gushed forth. Taichi laughed as well.

"It was pretty fancy, back then. There's no way they would have let us stay here for five thousand yen. It was a members-only kind of place."

"Oh?"

"My mom always likes to think of herself as being specially chosen. My brother too, probably."

Natsuko glanced toward her husband. He kept his gaze fixed on the TV, not realizing that she was looking at him.

"They're a little strange, those two, aren't they?" he said.

"Do you think so? When I was little, I thought it would still be possible to return to the good old days that my mom and all the others always talked about. But then after I came to this rundown hotel as a girl, I realized that the past isn't somewhere you can go back to. So I wasn't able to bring myself to come here again until now."

Taichi turned toward her. "Then what made you change your mind?"

"I don't know."

"It *is* pretty relaxing here, though," he said, before stuffing his little finger in his ear, and turning back to the TV. He let out a truly pleasure-filled laugh, quite as if he had completely forgotten their present conversation.

The sound of the TV enveloped her as she closed her eyes, leaving her feeling as if she were drifting off to sleep in their familiar apartment.

* * *

The next morning, Natsuko woke up before Taichi. As

she softly pulled back the curtain, a hard, cement-like ocean spread out before her. If she were to follow that sea northward, and keep going, she might end up at the coastal town where Taichi had been born. But in front of her, there was only the sea, stretching out to the horizon. A dark, leaden color, a lead mixed with the color of ash, a lead bordering on white. A color that couldn't be expressed in a single word. She felt confused. Wasn't her own past, like that sea, something that couldn't be put into words? Wasn't it precisely that violent force that had attacked her all of a sudden? Afraid, she squeezed her eyes shut, when she heard a voice carry across from behind her. "We'd better go get breakfast." She slowly opened her eyes.

Once they finished eating, Natsuko hurried Taichi back to their room. They packed their bags in a hurry, before going down to the front desk to finish checking out. Seeing as they still had a little time before the shuttle bus left, they decided to take a look at the souvenir corner.

Taichi walked around with his cane, sticking his nose into some sachets of herb potpourris like a bee collecting pollen. He floated around aimlessly, muttering his impressions of each of them in turn: "This one smells like sweets. This one's like black tea. And this one, this one smells like you, Natchan, like a newborn. Yep, this one's the best." He bought around a dozen different varieties.

"Who are you planning to give them to?"

"You know, there's Yoshimura, the orthopedic nurse, and Itō, the rehabilitation doctor." He listed a half-dozen or so names, even some that Natsuko didn't recognize. He spent most of his days at home, but it seemed that he had his own world too.

They were the only passengers to board the shuttlebus. The hotel faded into the distance behind them.

If the past had already been chewed to exhaustion, was there any point in continuing this journey? Natsuko let out a tired sigh.

"This really does smell just like you, Natchan," Taichi said, sniffing at the potpourri in the seat beside her.

* * *

They changed buses, and headed toward an art museum. Natsuko didn't want the journey to end just yet. She wanted to find some kind of healing, at least. She wanted to see the things that others considered beautiful. Some vague part of her felt that if she could look at those things for herself, she too might be able to think of them in that way. Maybe then she would be able to find some degree of peace. Taichi didn't question her sudden desire to visit the art gallery. He remained silent, as if he were happy simply to be there with her.

Natsuko supported her stumbling husband as they entered the building and approached a woman at the information desk. *Do you have a wheelchair?* Taichi asked, and without even waiting for her to respond, added: *Can I borrow one? My wife will push it.*

To Natsuko, his manner was as brazen as ever, but the woman didn't seem to be bothered by it. Once the wheelchair was brought his way, Taichi settled himself comfortably in the seat, and Natsuko began to slowly push him toward the galleries.

The first thing that she laid eyes on was an *objet d'art*, something that looked like a ball of yarn. It was round and seemed like it would be strangely warm to the touch. She tried to imagine whether people felt at peace when looking at such round warmth.

The next item was a landscape painting. The scene looked like an ornamental garden. There were flowers in every color imaginable, and trees bathed in light, casting long shadows over the lawn. She looked at the artist's name, the title of the painting, the year in which it had been produced, and tried to call to mind the ideas that the painter must have been trying express, and the thoughts and feelings that the picture must bring to those who looked at it.

They followed the path through the gallery, looking first at one image, then the next. After a short while, they came to a small picture.

It was a family portrait. There were two small children, a gaunt father, and a fat mother who was pouring milk into a cup. Natsuko confronted that scene—and as she did so, the past, which should already have been chewed to exhaustion, came rushing back. She thought about her own life, doubtful that the kind of scene depicted in the work, a family as peaceful as the one staring back at her, could ever truly exist. She doubted too whether anyone could ever eat so modestly.

Let's go to an expensive restaurant, the most expensive place you can imagine, she remembered a man saying to her once. This was after she had graduated from university, during her time as a temporary worker. She had been invited by a full-time employee at her company. Since Natsuko was a modest and docile woman, he must have thought that she wouldn't say anything, that he could get away with his sexual harassment, that seeing as he was her superior, she wouldn't be able to do anything about it. Eventually, his advances grew so persistent that she was forced to leave her job.

It was her mother who first realized what had happened. She kept pestering Natsuko, demanding to know why she had quit. More than anything, she was afraid of the idea of her daughter not working. Whether this was because both she and her son were dependent on Natsuko's income, or whether she wanted her daughter to have a successful career, Natsuko didn't know. She tried to explain that everything was okay, because she was looking for a new job now, but nothing would soothe her mother's temper. And having worked herself into a frenzy, her mother ended up striking her. So Natsuko had no choice but to tell her the truth. Not to stop the violence, but to calm her down, to cool her anger however she could. But her mother never considered the possibility that Natsuko had been targeted because of her average looks. She had convinced herself that her daughter was just too attractive, so like herself, and that was why she had been the victim of sexual harassment, until at last she wound up convincing herself that *she* was the victim, not her daughter.

She grasped Natsuko's hand tenderly. "I can't believe that someone would do such a terrible thing to you . . . It's unforgivable. We'll have to sue."

A court battle would be too hard on her, Natsuko said, trying to steer her away from the idea. Her mother took this so poorly that she slammed her fist down on the table.

"What's wrong with you? Why won't you do anything for me? All I want is some money. I'm so miserable. Can't you see that? What did I do to deserve such an inconsiderate child? Why are you always like this? Don't you love me? You're my daughter!" The promise of money that flickered before her eyes for a moment, only to vanish in a puff of smoke. That was her mother's greatest hate, the thought that got her most worked up.

"Stop it!" Natsuko pleaded desperately, but her mother slapped her with the flat of her hand. She tried desperately to pull away, but her mother's attack wouldn't stop, and Natsuko, in terror, cried out: "Get away from me!" She threw a nearby cushion and tissue box at her, struggling to put some distance between them. But then her mother grabbed her, and the two of them began to grapple with one another.

At that moment, her brother raised his voice in a frenzied cry, and started smashing first one windowpane, then the next. When he got like this, neither mother nor daughter could bring him under control. The feeling of indignation that had been churning inside Natsuko, that her mother ought to be aware on some level at least of her insatiable avarice, became cloudy and diluted.

The world in which the court case went forward felt unreal to Natsuko. The man, the full-time employee, seemed to have finally realized what he had done, and immediately offered to settle out of court. But, he said, he still loved her, and he insisted that she would have to accept the money in person at his attorney's law firm.

She met with the attorney at his office in Aoyama.

"I'm sorry to have to do things this way," he said. "Please accept my client's sincerest apologies. He wanted to ensure that you received it safely."

The attorney offered her an envelope. It passed before her eyes, to her mother, who put it in her handbag. Her brother glared at their mother, as if muttering to himself:

"That isn't *yours*." He wasn't even trying to hide it. Finally, they parted ways with the attorney, and her mother said drunkenly: "Let's get a taxi."

The car passed through the streets of Aoyama before stopping in front of a familiar building. The driver followed her brother's instructions. Natsuko said nothing. She had known from the very beginning that it would come to this.

It was a famous Chinese restaurant. Her mother ordered one dish after the other—Peking duck, chili sauce prawns, *okoge*—seeming to relish each and every one of them. Her younger brother ordered a bottle of Shaoxing wine. The family sat in silence. Immersed in the food. Silence permeated only by the sound of eating. Neither of them had realized that they could only eat this way because she had been sexually harassed—that they were, in effect, celebrating her suffering. That unending, uninterrupted sound stirred up feelings of disgust in her, resounding again and again in her mind, aggravating her hearing, her nerves, her soul. She just wanted to lose consciousness, to collapse then and there. Not only had the man sexually harassed her—now, her family was tormenting her even more.

Natsuko didn't know which it was that disgusted her more, the man or the sight of her younger brother sipping that Shaoxing wine. She herself didn't understand what it was that was hurting her. The series of events surrounding the harassment all converged, and ever since then, she found herself often visited by unpleasant experiences that she couldn't put into words. And she started to refer to that convergence of events as *that life*.

And yet it was in the midst of *that life* that she met a man, Taichi, whom she decided to marry. She understood.

That there could be no erasing the memories of those blasphemies, no pretending that they had never existed. That the only thing that she could do was to combine her life with that of someone else—it didn't even matter if it wasn't a man—and try to dilute the past.

Maybe if she told Taichi about those blasphemies, he would understand. But what would happen, she wondered, if she tried to confide in him? About what had happened in that restaurant? About how heartily her mother and brother had been eating and drinking? About how unbearable that sound had been? Maybe he would understand, if she tried to tell him about it all, calmly, matter-of-factly. Yes, if she tried to speak to him about them now, he might just understand. *You hear about it a lot, don't you? About people who are able to go through their whole lives without ever complaining about anything. But you know, I don't know why, but I just can't hold it in anymore . . .* But if she said that, Taichi might absorb all her suffering. He might accept it all, every last drop of it. He might finally *understand.* It might leave him weeping, his nose running like a child's. So she said nothing. She didn't want to see such a sight—such a pure, thankful sight. Someone like herself, who had passed through *that life*, didn't deserve that kind of sympathy.

All of a sudden, Taichi let out a loud burp. "What's the matter?" Natsuko asked.

"I must have eaten too much at the buffet," he answered. She seemed to have been standing still, staring at that family portrait for quite some time. "Let's keep going," he urged her.

The next painting was of a ripe pomegranate placed on a wooden table. The vivid redness of the fruit was too lively, too warm. It grated against her heart, leaving her feeling painful and cramped. The next one, however, was an abstract painting that looked like some kind of three-dimensional object. She felt at once peaceful, relieved to have found something that she could look at with ease, something with a sense of distance.

In this way, as she stood in front of the pictures, she kept finding herself going through a cycle of fear and relief, over and over. When she felt at ease, and thought to herself that she wouldn't mind just standing in front of a certain work for a while, Taichi would urge her to take him to the next one. And it would almost certainly be some terrible picture, something made of complex intersections of straight lines that made her think of young men, like her brother. She wanted to run away from such images as fast as she could, but no matter what the picture, Taichi would examine them all carefully, in the same deliberate way. And yet not once did he voice his impressions. "Let's keep going," was all he said.

Next, they came to a self-portrait. "Oh!" exclaimed Taichi, leaning forward in the wheelchair. Natsuko didn't know the first thing about self-portraits. Could it be that her husband had an eye for them? She knew that he was good at drawing. He cherished the manga that he had written as a child. And the sketches that he had done during his art classes were indeed quite splendid. She stood in silence behind her husband as they looked at the self-portrait. It was filled with color, temperature, and movement. Ah, she thought, *this* is a person.

"Let's keep going," Taichi said again. She pushed the wheelchair toward the next picture. It was a still life depicting various flowers of different colors. She had seen women holding such flowers but had never bought any herself. She stared into the picture, thinking that it too was probably something that people considered beautiful. It didn't look particularly beautiful to her, but surely it must have appeared that way to others. When she stopped to think about it, it seemed so obvious that one's own feelings are of course different to those of others, but only now did she understand. It was unnatural to look for healing in what others, but not she herself, considered beautiful. But, she thought, if the people around her thought that it was beautiful, that didn't have to bother her. Now wasn't the time to go chasing after what she herself considered beautiful. Things that were beautiful, things that were just—she wanted to take a break from them all for a while. While she had always had some awareness of the unnaturalness of what she was doing, up until now she had never paused to reflect on it all. Or rather, she had always been stuck waiting for an opportunity to give voice to these feelings of contradiction and unreasonableness.

Her heart was distressed one moment, calm the next, continuously being tossed around by the waves. The unrestful things that disturbed her and the things that brought her assurance could be found in equal measure in each and every picture. She witnessed them all, together with Taichi, flowing together as a single current. They didn't move in front of the pictures—rather, the paintings seemed to float up in front of them. First one, then the next, one after the other, filling her heart with all kinds of impressions, before quickly sinking back into the stream. She no longer paid attention to the artists' names, nor to the titles, nor to the years in which they had been produced. She simply watched as the paintings flowed by in turn. After a while, the vivid impressions reached out to her only for the briefest of moments—until at last no sooner might a picture awaken some deep-rooted feeling inside her than it would slip quietly into the past. She no longer felt afraid. There were paintings that were difficult to understand, that were creepy, or discomforting—but she was able to look at them, just look at them, directly, while at the same time still being oblivious to any deeper meaning that might lie within. And as she looked at these images that conveyed no meaning, she realized that she had broken out of that state of mind in which looking was unbearable. Now, she could face them all, even without understanding. She was simply looking at pictures.

She didn't associate them with anything anymore. There wasn't anything left to be afraid of. Not her mother, nor her younger brother. She felt nothing.

They came flowing back to her. *Your grandfather, you know.* The words with which her mother would always begin that heroic saga.

Your grandfather, you know, he took us to all these hotels in a hired car driven by a chauffeur.

On arriving at each hotel, Natsuko's mother, her grandfather's beloved daughter, would inspect the suite. If she didn't like it, they would all get back into the hired car and go somewhere else. And the health retreat was the place that she liked the most. Wearing a dress, dancing in the salon with Natsuko's grandfather and grandmother. French cuisine at an ocean-view restaurant. Chanson performances. Each of those things had made her young mother feel special.

It was strange, Natsuko thought. Now, she could picture her mother's stories, those stories that she had so detested, with indifference, as though they belonged to someone else. Her mother's agitated way of talking, where you could almost see her tongue darting around, was indeed unpleasant, but now it was just an image, one picture among many. She could look at her pitiable mother, she could see her as part of a portrait of a wealthy family. And she could look at that scene without calling to mind the regret that her mother, completely unawares, must have felt when she contemplated that special time now past. If she did that, Natsuko realized, she could look at them as no more than memories of a vacation taken by a rather ordinary, well-to-do family.

Eventually, her mother had been forced to give up her property, to part with her apartment in order to pay off her son's debts, and to move with him to the suburbs. There, after catching wind of the rumors that she had fled to the countryside in shame, she ended up trying to kill herself. She spent a week in hospital. Then, no sooner had she been discharged than she started running to the local psychiatrist, clinging to her doctors, shedding fake tears, pretending to have aphasia, all in a bid for sympathy, all in an attempt to convince someone, anyone, that she should receive a disability pension. It should have been much easier for her just to find a job, but her mother didn't see things that way. And so instead, she tried to get her hands on money the only way that she knew how. But of course, even if she had succeeded, it would only have ended up feeding her son's alcoholism.

Her mother, however, had no such apprehensions, and kept on going as if nothing were amiss. She felt no sense of danger at the possibility of going broke, of finding herself completely penniless. She spent her days decorating her new suburban apartment with lace in all her favorite colors, pale pinks and whites. Her small, meagre castle. A castle in which even the darkness was bleached white. The room was fitted with a bed surrounded by a canopy of pure white lace. The pillows were like blue and pink heart-shaped marshmallows, as if even they were divided into male and female, like pairs of lovers. She passed the days sleeping in that huge bed, so soft that it was as if her body would sink into it and disappear. She resembled nothing so much as a pistil in the center of a rose.

Right, Natsuko remembered, her father too had been good at drawing.

When her mother finally had to let go of her apartment, she let Natsuko sort through her deceased father's belongings. Her mother cherished that 8 mm film, but she was completely indifferent toward her late husband's things, telling her daughter that if she wanted them, she could keep them, that if she didn't, she could throw them out.

As she sifted through them all, Natsuko felt for the first time as if she truly understood her father.

Among those items, she came across an old diary. Her father, it seemed, had been a student at a vocational high school. She found herself filled with curiosity at what he had studied there. The only thing that her mother had ever told her about him, at least of the time before he came down with his disease, was that he had held an office job at a prestigious company. And that, as such, she had been incredibly happy when they got engaged. *After he proposed, I quit my job as a stewardess, of course, so I'd go to see plays at the theater with your grandmother. I was so happy. I didn't have to do anything anymore, I could just go and watch the plays, doing nothing. It was like soaking in a nice, warm bath, forever. It was so wonderful. I got married, bought an apartment to live in, and kept living like that for a while. I was so shocked at how much money I had, I was able to save so much. So I thought to myself, why don't I buy another apartment with all these savings?*

That was what her mother thought. That she could rent out another apartment, that she could earn money without working. But before she could buy that second apartment, her husband was felled by illness. And not long after, she had been forced to sell off her one and only apartment to pay for her son's debts, left with no choice but to move to the suburbs. Her happiness, like a warm bath, didn't last.

That was why, no doubt, her mother didn't want her deceased husband's belongings.

Natsuko found some pictures amid those items. He must have drawn them during his days at the vocational school. The first was a sketch of a Van Gogh painting, the second a landscape. They both had notes on the back, one giving a mark of eighty points, and the other ninety. Her father, it seemed, had been an outstanding student.

There was even a picture that had received a full hundred points. It was a delicate abstract sketch, almost mechanical, like the interlocked gears inside a clock. Black, grey, white. Each gear was drawn in monochrome gradations, but no matter which she looked at, not a single one of them was the same shade as any other. She didn't know whether it was a beautiful picture. But she could tell that it was a very elaborate one, one that must have required a high level of skill to draw. So this was the kind of picture that scored a hundred points, she wondered in admiration.

It was a premonition, she thought, of the mysterious

disease that would attack her father's brain, the brain of a worker at a prestigious company, and leave him with dementia. And it was also, it seemed to Natsuko, a premonition of her mother's life, a life that should have turned out so differently, and the final unexpected downfall of a family that stretched back to the time of her grandfather.

It wasn't that the gears were broken and in total disarray—rather, they looked to be frozen at the point just before collapse, faded into monochrome, and fitted into a sheet of paper. At the moment when, if just one more second were to elapse, the teeth would fail to mesh together, and the whole mechanism would shatter before one's eyes.

She spent a long time looking at that sketch, staring at it as if it had nothing at all to do with her family.

In the end, she looked at all the works. She experienced each of them in turn.

They left the wheelchair in the place marked by the exit. Taichi seemed disappointed to part with it.

This journey had only been for herself, Natsuko thought, feeling beholden to her husband.

"Do you want to go anywhere else?" she asked.

"How about the beach?" Taichi suggested.

* * *

They followed the footpath that ran along the shoreline, the wind blowing around them. Natsuko could smell the salty air wafting up from the sea.

Taichi, out of nowhere, said: "I'm taking a test for an electric wheelchair tomorrow. So I wanted to get used to sitting in one."

"Oh, really?"

Natsuko helped him down to the beach. He stabbed at the sand with his cane, confirming his footing as he ambled forward.

Some children ran up from behind, overtaking them. Taichi came to a stop, and watched the children run past. "How cute," he murmured to himself, before turning to Natsuko. "I'll be able to get one with a nickel battery. It's got awesome horsepower. That's what they're going to let me use. I can get it for a ten percent copayment with the welfare office. Pretty lucky, huh?"

A stray dog approached them. Taichi crouched down, trying to pat it on the head, but he was unable to bend over properly, and so instead flashed it a broad smile. The dog turned around and ran ahead along the beach.

"I can't keep up with kids, or dogs, can I? It'll be different when I get the wheelchair."

"What should I do? Do you want me to go with you?" Natsuko asked, feeling more devoted than ever.

"You don't have to do anything, Natchan. With the wheelchair, *I'll* carry *your* stuff," he said, leaning against her.

The waves brushed at their feet. Thinking that Taichi would get wet, Natsuko pushed him lightly up the slope, but he fell down. She offered him her hand, but he couldn't stand up.

"With the wheelchair, we'll be able to go overseas. Anywhere we want, right?" In his excitement, Taichi spread his hands wide as if to emphasize the word *anywhere*.

The waves broke over him the moment he finished speaking. Natsuko sat beside him. She wasn't worried about getting wet. She wanted to hear the sound of the waves a little longer.

They watched the sea in silence. It was the usual silence that fell over them.

The sea was constantly changing shape, like something whose true form could never be truly grasped.

She began to think about the things that she had long considered incomprehensible. About why Taichi never asked her why her family treated him so poorly, about why his neurological disease had befallen him. What did he think about that long series of unreasonableness and contradiction? But now, at the end of their trip, she finally felt as if she understood. He didn't think about them at all. Taking off one's clothes on a warm day, putting up an umbrella on a rainy one—that was the extent of his thoughts. Like someone reflecting on the changing seasons, and saying: *Ah, it's warming up.* Like someone who after being exposed to violence of every kind decided simply to take a brief rest. That was how he lived. Anyone else would no doubt have been fed up with it all, with the unfairness of everything. But Taichi wasn't like that. Of course, unfairness still existed in his world—but he just swallowed it down whole. No matter how bad it was, no matter how poisonous.

But what about herself? Natsuko wondered. How should *she* deal with her life, with *that life*? She wasn't her husband. What could *she* do?

The waves surged forward. A sense of dread came over her, that they would keep rushing toward her forever. Because she couldn't make out their true form.

The seascape began to blur. She felt tears welling in her eyes. "When I was little," she began, "I always thought the sea was so scary. Why, I wonder . . . ?"

Taichi said nothing.

She turned around, only to see her husband spread out like a star, sound asleep with his stomach peeking out from the bottom of his shirt.

His belly looking up at the sky, his thighs opened out to the sea, his breathing, like the waves, keeping to the same slow, gentle rhythm.

She pulled his shirt down to cover his navel.

As she stared at his sleeping face, Natsuko began to reflect on how she had used the words *unreasonable* and *contradiction* to describe *that life. I don't get it, that way of thinking,* she thought she heard Taichi say.

She remembered something that he had said to her once: *I've known the sea since I was a kid. The tide is always rising and falling.*

No doubt he had never feared it. Natsuko was afraid of things changing. She was terrified of it, in the same way that she was terrified of violence. And the sea was no different. But Taichi seemed to have no such fear. He had always been like that. To him, no doubt, the whole world was made up of a constant tide of rising and falling.

He was a special person, Natsuko thought as she watched him lying there on the sand. A special person— someone she had never seen before, someone she had just seen for the first time in her life. But it was a strange kind of specialness. Even sitting beside that special person, she felt no sense of envy. But then, on the other hand, she felt no sense of superiority at being the wife of such a special person either. She just knew that she had picked up something very important. It was something that she had been given to look after for a while, something that, when the time came, she would have to give back.

To Natsuko, this man, fast asleep with his belly exposed to the water, seemed also to be asleep to the wide, open sea of unreasonableness that comprised the world.

Without seizing on the identity of her feelings, her sense of not properly belonging in her family, Natsuko, in her constant state of anxiety, had made a truly spur-of-the-moment decision to bring this stranger into her life. Her family's illness would infect him too, and consume him from within, she thought. He would be a hapless victim, but it was her fate to find a necessary sacrifice, so there was no way of helping it. He would ultimately end up being absorbed by her family, by *that life*. That was what she had believed.

When she looked back on it all, it was a strange, miraculous turn of events. A thorny ivy of arrogance and waste, built up over three generations, had entwined itself around her, trying to rob her of her very soul. And it had been swept away in an instant thanks to one average man's cerebral attack. She wondered whether he really was so pitiful. If not for those seizures, he would have been destined to have everything he ever had be torn away from him by her family. He had managed to avoid that fate in a way that no one could have foreseen. Indeed, the attacks had begun with exquisite timing, without even the slightest margin of error. Quite as if they had been lying dormant in wait from the very beginning. Natsuko had found no means of her own to escape from her family. And Taichi—he was a simple, good-natured person, the kind of person who, even feeling ill at ease around his wife's family, even knowing that they were exploiting him, would give them every last ounce of what he had. This was the kind of couple that the cerebral attacks had fallen on. It was an attack on their very lives.

The wind was growing colder.

Natsuko woke her husband, and they went back the way they had come. She looked at the footprints that he left in the sand. He dragged his feet when he walked, so his tracks stretched longer than normal.

They returned to the plaza in front of the station.

Why don't we try out the foot bath? It's gotten cold, don't you think? Natsuko said. *What foot bath?* Taichi tilted his head. *Come on,* she urged, nudging him along.

Several people were sitting there with their legs submerged. Steam was rising from the water. *What's this?* Taichi asked. *You can put your feet in,* Natsuko answered. *Come on, it'll feel good.*

Do you want to go in? a woman asked them. *Does it cost anything?* Taichi responded. *No, it's free, but the towels do. You can buy one if you want, but you don't have to.*

Let's buy one, Natsuko said. *I took one from the hotel, so we're okay,* Taichi answered. *It'll make a good memento,* she insisted.

She wanted to buy something for her husband, no matter how trivial it was, no matter how unnecessary to their lives. But he hadn't realized that. He would probably never realize it—or maybe, after several years, she would finally find herself able to tell him everything.

She couldn't enter the foot bath with him. If she didn't hold onto him, he might lose his balance, and fall over backward. So she decided to support him. It was the sensible thing to do.

Taichi took off his shoes and socks. Natsuko and the woman helped support him. He slowly dipped his legs into the water, one by one, and sat down.

Wow, it's so warm! Taichi shone her a fully satisfied

smile. He didn't question for a second whether she would soak her feet too. That was fine.

Is something wrong, Mister? the woman asked. Taichi nodded. It was only Natsuko's family who condemned him for the way his body was, and he made no effort to hide his disability. *What's wrong?* she asked again. *My brain,* Taichi answered. *Oh my, your brain, that's awful,* the woman said, feigning surprise. *There's an electrode in my brain. The battery's attached to my chest,* Taichi continued. *Really? There's a machine here?* The woman touched his chest. Taichi nodded, letting the woman leave her hand there. *Really, there's a machine here . . . Oh my, yes, here it is.* Taichi laughed, as if being tickled. He looked to be enjoying himself.

He was always on the move, always pushing his body in spite of his disability. He wasn't able to help himself, always going out to buy sweets, manga, adult DVDs, and the like. And now he had set himself on the idea—and not a bad one at that—of buying an electric wheelchair. It was no doubt that unwavering drive to action that had spread to Natsuko, that had prompted her to set out on this trip in pursuit of her family's lingering regrets, chasing after things that couldn't be looked on directly.

"Where are we going now?" Taichi asked innocently.

"We'll take the bullet train home. We're finished here."

"There isn't anywhere else you want to go?"

"No. There's nowhere else to go. Nothing left to see. Nothing at all."

Taichi sat in silence for a while, staring off into the distance, likely still unable to comprehend the meaning that lay behind those words.

Even if she explained to him that it was all over, all

finished, he still wouldn't understand. So Natsuko said nothing.

The bullet train began to slide out under that sky, too ripe in color to properly call dusk, as the two of them left the sea.

Taichi pulled out a handful of tissues. He used them to blow his nose with all his strength, before rolling them into a ball and stuffing them back into his pocket. To Natsuko, watching on beside him, he seemed to resemble nothing so much as a figure who had taken the various joys and sufferings of life, put them all into one picture after another, rolled them all up, and stuffed them deep into his pocket.

She felt herself overcome by a sense of awe at her husband's actions. And then she asked, as if the words had been bubbling up inside her all along: *Was the foot bath good?* He nodded. *Was the trip fun?* He nodded again. *Do you want to go to somewhere else some time, together?* Taichi paused for a while, seemingly deep in thought, before nodding once more.

He didn't say anything, merely watching the scenery flow by. But he had indeed nodded to each of her questions.

The two of them sat in silence for a while. Eventually, the in-car sales trolley began to make its way down the aisle. But Natsuko wasn't paying attention. If she had been her usual self, she might have been driven by a sense of self-sacrifice, a force that might be described as almost sensual, to buy her husband a snack of mixed nuts or something like that.

The short journey was nearing its end. *Hey, what exactly do you see in that man?* came her mother's voice. *You don't honestly think he's handsome, do you?* But

Natsuko couldn't really explain what she liked about him, not in words. Her mother, every now and then, would say, her voice dripping with sarcasm: *What an unfortunate man. Such a shame. Coming down with that disease, but still clinging onto life. Unable to work, having to be taken care of by his wife all the time. The nerve.* At such times, Natsuko would be secretly grateful that she had married him.

The skyscrapers of Tokyo came into sight. She could even make out a luxury hotel where she had once stayed using her brother's credit card. Her mother probably didn't even remember that card anymore. For her, only the happy memories remained. *That son of mine is so terribly filial, he even invited me to go with him to a truly wonderful hotel,* she had said once. She probably didn't even remember that he had gotten involved in a huge fight at the bar that time either. Or the trouble that had ensued after her attempted suicide, when she had been forced to let go of her apartment. Natsuko couldn't tell whether the sense of oblivion that visited her mother was a form of enlightenment, or whether she had merely turned her eyes away from reality. All she knew was that, as far she herself was concerned, a certain season had passed. All thanks to the attacks of the man beside her, this man sitting there rolling tissues into balls.

"What's for dinner?" Taichi asked.

Natsuko pondered the question for a moment. She hadn't thought that far ahead. She was tired, so whatever she was going to cook, she wanted to get it over and done with quickly. All they had left in the kitchen was a bunch of bean sprouts, a few eggs, and the butter that Taichi's mother had sent them from Hokkaido. It was unmistakably butter, not margarine. That and a little bit of brown rice.

"How about we buy some *shimeji* mushrooms from that hundred-yen store near the station and make a risotto?"

"Oh? I love risotto."

The bullet train was approaching Tokyo Station. Her journey was nearing its end. She felt vaguely tired. When she leaned against Taichi's body, he turned to glance at her face for a second, his eyes blinking in puzzlement.

* * *

Taichi's electric wheelchair test took place the following day. A public health nurse from the welfare office, a young man called Nakayama, came to their apartment. He was a little tactless, his attitude that of someone fresh out of university. As he helped Taichi into a manual wheelchair, he kept telling him over and over how much he loved him, treating him like a younger brother despite his being the elder.

The test would be at the Shinjuku Ward Disability Welfare Center. It was a bit of a distance, the nurse explained, near the last stop on the streetcar line.

Taichi, however, looked happy.

The nurse pushed the wheelchair down the road. Judging by the conversation, Taichi seemed to have already met him several times before. And of course, he showed not the slightest hint of humility or embarrassment.

The three of them boarded the streetcar. Taichi kept on asking all kinds of questions. From what he and the nurse were saying, it sounded like it would be a practical test. When Natsuko asked what would happen if her husband failed, the nurse responded only by saying that it shouldn't be too difficult, that so long as Taichi didn't bump the wheelchair into anyone, he would pass.

Taichi and the nurse were still talking when they arrived at the Disability Welfare Center. The three of them sat through all the formal procedures, followed by an interview with a doctor, before finally moving on to the test. Natsuko watched over her husband from behind as the wheelchair began to move.

The test was more difficult than she had expected. As he made his way up the hill and across the road at the pedestrian lights, Taichi seemed about to bump into the myriad passersby more times than Natsuko could count.

They didn't have to wait long for the results. *Why don't we practice a little more?* the examiner said. In other words, Taichi had failed. However, he would still be able to use the electric wheelchair so long as he had someone accompanying him, and from the sound of it, they would still be able to buy one. Taichi didn't seem particularly disappointed, but the nurse insisted on trying to comfort him, telling him over and over again that it wasn't a disastrous outcome.

One month later, the electric wheelchair finally arrived. They set it up in the bicycle lot next to their apartment building. *Shall we leave it here? You're a big guy, so we had to have it custom-made,* the clerk from the nursing care equipment shop told Taichi. The seat was fitted with a large, soft cushion, an optional add-on that Taichi seemed to have ordered without consulting his wife. That was just like him. There was no mistaking, however, that it looked comfortable to sit in.

"Have a go," Natsuko urged him.

Taichi lowered himself into the seat, before quickly taking off and driving in circles around her.

"With this, I'll be able to go and buy sweets in no time at all!" Taichi exclaimed, brimming with excitement.

"You'll just go and buy more of those dirty magazines, won't you? You can't fool me."

Taichi let out a joyous laugh. "But what about you, Natchan? Do you want anything?"

"Anything that I want?" Natsuko fell silent. She had no idea what she wanted. She had never stopped to ask herself that question.

"I can go shopping now, so let me know, and I'll buy it for you," Taichi said proudly. The words sounded to Natsuko as if he had come up with the most splendid plan. She could get whatever she wanted. She could do whatever she wanted.

"I . . ." Natsuko began, "I want to watch TV with you."

"TV? Hmm . . ." Taichi paused for a moment, pondering. "That's it! I'll buy a TV guide! It's almost March, so there'll be a special edition with all the new shows! Speaking of which, Natchan, your mind's always somewhere else, huh?"

"That sounds good. Yes, please buy one."

It looked like he had seen through her.

"I picked up a lot of these. Can you hold onto them?"

He was holding out several packets of pocket tissues labelled with advertisements, the kind that were handed out in front of the station. She put them into the pocket of her apron.

Natsuko still didn't really know whether she could say what she wanted, or go out and buy it. That was why she had given him such a timid answer. But she could see now that that was the cause of everything. She tried to put into words, even if only in a whisper, the miserableness of her past. And those words seemed to bring a strange sense of healing. Her apron pocket had begun to swell, but there was still plenty of room for more tissues.

"I'll be back soon," Taichi said. And with that, he took off out of the bicycle lot. He was supposed to be accompanied by someone, but he didn't let that worry him.

As she saw her husband off, her mobile began to ring with a call from her mother.

"You haven't called in so long. Did something happen? I was really lonely, you know."

"Oh. I came down a cold."

"I found some more new clothes. They looked so wonderful, so lovely. I sent them to you."

They're so soft and fluffy, reaching all the way down to the hem, and fluttering around so mesmerizingly.

Natsuko thanked her before hanging up. She had finally realized that she didn't have to wear them, that she had that option too.

When she looked up again, Taichi was making his way down the street, cutting a clean path through the stream of people, straighter and faster than anyone else.

Ninety-Nine Kisses

I opened my eyes with rapture. What a wonderful dream! Meiko, Moeko, Yōko, and me. All four of us, joining hands in a circle. Our palms getting all hot and sweaty and clingy. Our bodies melting into a thick syrup, becoming one. We were one. Meiko's pain was Moeko's suffering. When some burning, fluorescent light pierced my sister's hearts, my body too shuddered with pain. This was what I had always yearned for. I don't know why I've always wanted to become one with them. It's instinctive. It's desire, that's all, pure and simple. Flowery words can't justify it. I'm just completely enamored with them.

Meiko, Moeko, Yōko, I thought, chanting their names like some kind of love spell. Words have power, even by themselves. That's why I don't say them very much. Words like *love*, or *death*. Whenever I recite the names of my three sisters, I find myself drifting off into a deep fog. Even at college the other day, during a lecture about Marcel Pagnol, I wasn't really paying attention to whatever my French professor, Monsieur Kimura, was saying. I just sat in my seat, repeating the names of my beloved sisters to myself over and over, writing them down again and again in my notebook.

"Sounds like a sister complex to me," my classmate Tamura said when we went to Hanake to get a bite to eat.

"A complex? That's rich. You say that like it's some kind of sickness, loving your sisters. And what with *your* mother complex."

"That's completely different. All I do is put up with that old bag's nagging. But you, you've pretty much gone and offered up your own guts to your sisters in sacrifice."

Tamura may well have been right about that. "That's a good one, coming from you." I smiled. "But I guess there might be times when I *do* want to offer up my heart to them, or my shit-stained guts, even if they don't want them. Anyway, how long do you think those jumbo *gyōza* are going to take?"

"You sure eat a lot, don't you? At this rate, you really will be able to offer them some shit-stained guts. Your breath already reeks of garlic."

Tamura and I often go out to eat garlic dishes like this. He's the kind of guy who always acts calm and indifferent, no matter what's going on, who goes around wearing worn-out T-shirts, his hair covered in dandruff. Basically, he's the kind of guy that girls call gross. On top of that, he's always coming out with these macho comments, like that there's no helping women who can't play the piano. But Tamura himself knows that he's like this, and the fact that he doesn't really think of me as a woman actually puts me at ease. That's why I had decided to hang out with him.

"So? Haven't you ever thought about shutting that bitch up?" I asked. "You could finish her off, you know?"

"She's an old bag, not a bitch. Anyway, I'm not going to kill her, if that's what you mean. It'd be too much of a hassle to clean up. By the way, the *gyōza* here are pretty big, aren't they?"

"I've been coming here with my family ever since I was

a kid. All I'd have to do is go for a walk around Nippori, and as soon as I'd pass by this place, I'd just get incredibly hungry, you know? So I'd end up getting some *gyōza* and a bowl of shaved ice to snack on."

"*Gyōza* and shaved ice? What a combination."

"Right? My sisters have it when they come here too. We're all big eaters. By the way, if you're having trouble dealing with that old bag, why not try asking that *tsukudani* store around here to help out? You can make *tsukudani* from just about anything, you know."

Tamura let out a disgusted sigh. "How can you say that about someone's mother? And you call yourself a woman?"

"I don't know. I mean, I've been brought up like a boy ever since I was little. Whenever there was a festival, they wouldn't let me ride on the float. They made me carry the *mikoshi* with all the boys. That's what my family's like."

"The float, huh? I've always had a thing for the girls riding on top of that."

This time, it was my turn to let out a disgusted sigh. "Everyone works so hard to pull it through the streets, but it's always the girls sitting at the top who capture everyone's hearts." But then I realized that Tamura was probably just acting macho, so I let him be.

* * *

When I got home, my sisters were all gossiping about this guy called S whom we had seen at the Azalea Festival at Nezu Shrine. He had only just moved into the neighborhood, but my sisters had already fallen for him. I had happened to see him myself not too long ago too, over at the Mad Hat. Everyone else was drinking Jinro, but then there he was, the odd one out with that Bloody Caesar of his. The Mad Hat. A run-down drinking house in the middle of this Shitamachi, this laid-back low town nestled in the old-fashioned, earthy half of Tokyo far from the bustle and commotion of the Yamanote. And this smug, pretentious-looking outsider sipping at his cocktail. He clearly didn't belong here. He could probably spend the rest of his life in this Shitamachi bar, and would still never find a way to fit in.

When I saw him at the Azalea Festival, he was empty-handed, as if he hadn't expected all the food stands to be there. He must have come just to see the flowers, never mind that you have to pay to go in. My sisters and I had been completely oblivious to those flowers ever since we were kids, and were busy stuffing ourselves with *takoyaki* and cotton candy.

"Didn't he say the azaleas were so pretty? He must be a flower person," Meiko said.

"I don't know about that. He might have just been putting on airs. But that kind of naivety is so cute, don't you think?" Moeko replied.

The two of them couldn't stop talking about him.

I looked at Yōko. She had always had a cunning streak, ever since she was small. I was probably the only one of us capable of loving her unconditionally. I could see her eyes burning with jealousy as she listened to Meiko and Moeko go on and on. Knowing that two of her sisters wanted him too, she was no doubt plotting to make a move of her own. She may have been pretending to ignore them, but I'll bet that she was planning to give him a flower or something behind their backs. Because that's the kind of person she is.

When we saw him that time at the Azalea Festival, we quickly learned that he was around the same age as Meiko. And when she realized that, Meiko's face turned bright red for some reason. Did she think that she had a chance with him just because they were so close in years? It looked like Moeko had thought the same thing too. She made a face, as if she found it all kind of boring. Yōko just watched on coolly. After all, she knew that men preferred younger women. None of them had any way of knowing whether S was even interested in them, but love has a way of making people get big-headed like that.

"You were the only one who said anything to him, weren't you? He looked a little flustered," Moeko insisted.

"Not at all!" Meiko replied. "He sounded so happy, when we were talking together."

"I'm not so sure about that."

I looked back and forth between my three sisters. Each of these three women, in their own way, seemed to have found themselves developing a vague interest in this man who had popped up here from some faraway town. It was probably only a matter of time before they started fighting over him. I love them, all three of my sisters, but for some reason, cruel thoughts kept pouring into my mind. They should fight more, I thought. Because women are born to fight. At least that's the way that it has always seemed to me. I mean, I'm always paying attention to how my sisters smell. Everything from their perfumes and makeup when they go out, to the scent of menstrual blood that they leave in the bathroom when they're on their periods. And those scents must get even richer after getting into a fight. Just thinking about it was enough to send a shiver coursing through my flesh. I wanted those scents to be stronger, I wanted to be able to breathe them in and savor them. With men, there's simply no comparison. Men smell of nothing but sweat. They don't give off different scents depending on the time or place, the way that women do.

If jealousy is a feminine characteristic, then women ought to be free to be as jealous as they want. And a loving attachment to a jealous woman—there's no way that a man would be able to understand that.

Flowers bursting into bloom one after another, each their own distinct, burning color. It's as if they're all trying to cry out over the top of one another that they're the most beautiful. And these people who live around Nezu Shrine, they probably go there, to the Azalea Festival, hoping that they'll be able to meet someone or another, whether friends or members of the opposite sex. Everyone goes there to have fun, to socialize in the middle of that explosion of color, surrounded by flowers all vying for their attention. *Hello! How are you doing? It's already that time of year. Thank goodness the weather's fine.* They'll start by exchanging pleasantries, but maybe what they really want to say is something more. *What are you doing after this? Do you mind if I tag along? The thing is, I think I've fallen in love with you.*

And then they part ways. *Let's catch up again sometime.* Maybe that's what they say. But what's that supposed to mean? It isn't like they're never going to see each other again. They live in the same neighborhood, after all.

And the same thing went for my sisters. *Let's catch up again sometime,* they said to S as we parted ways. Of course they were thinking about seeing him again. They were probably all thinking the exact same thing. That next time, maybe they would find him somewhere around the Mad Hat. But there's one thing that they can't have been thinking. That someone else would end up getting their hands on him, this guy, this mysterious S. That one of their own sisters might make him her own boyfriend first. No, that thought couldn't have occurred to them at all.

* * *

One day, I happened to catch sight of S at the bus stop near our house. Well, technically it isn't really a bus stop. The place had something to do with the Bluestocking Society, the feminist literary group that used to be active around here a century ago. He was staring intently at the sign that described their connection to the local area. And then, completely out of nowhere, he went and kissed it. I was so surprised that I spun around to see whether anyone else had noticed. But it was still early in the morning, and there was no one else around. I was probably the only one who had seen it. After that, he headed off toward Hakusan, while I kept going toward the convenience store in the opposite direction. I went straight to the magazine shelves, looking through the latest editions of all my favorites. One of them was doing a special issue on the Printemps Ginza department store. I had wanted to take a look at the new selection of summer clothes, but as I flipped through the pages, I just couldn't relax. I couldn't get that picture of S kissing the sign out of my head.

In the end, I went home with only a carton of milk.

"You took your time," Meiko remarked. "Does it really take that long to buy some milk?"

"Uh, well . . ." I replied, flustered, probably just making myself look like I had done something wrong.

"You're a strange one," Moeko laughed.

She was probably right about that. And all the while, Yōko kept staring at me. I couldn't help but worry that she might somehow manage to see through my discomfort, so I ran upstairs to hide in my room. I couldn't tell any of them about what I had seen, about S kissing that sign. They would probably just end up getting jealous, I thought. They would no doubt just end up arguing among themselves over why he had done it.

My mind started wandering. Why *had* he kissed it? Did he feel some kind of reverence toward Hiratsuka Raichō? I could picture it so vividly. S, kissing my sisters against their will. My bookish sisters, who had so eagerly devoured the works of Uno Chiyo and Okamoto Kanoko back when they were kids. How would these sisters of mine feel if a pretentious guy, some outsider, came and pressed his lips up against their own? And what if he kissed me? I would slap him dead in the face. *Don't treat me like an idiot! Maybe it's true, that kissing someone, even without checking to see how they feel about you, maybe that's how things are done where the streets are ruled by the young. But this town isn't like that. The young aren't in charge here. So don't you get it? When in Rome, you're supposed to do as the Romans do.* Yep. If it were me, that's what I would say to him.

My sisters. My poor sisters. They haven't realized what exactly it is that draws them to him. If you ask me, it's simply because he's a stranger. They think that they're all so mature and sophisticated. They think that they've picked up every bit of worldly wisdom that a woman needs to know from their books. *I'm not going to marry a local, some childhood friend*, Moeko once said. *I'm not going to be like everyone else in this town. They're all the same. They're born here, they fall in love with a member of the opposite sex, someone they've known since elementary school, they get married, and then, eventually, they die. Then their childhood friends all come to the funeral, like it's some kind of class reunion. No, I couldn't bring myself to fall in love with someone like that. It's practically incest.* That's the kind of thing that Moeko would always say. Which was why, as soon as a stranger popped up, she and the others all underwent a sudden awakening, almost as if it were their first time ever seeing a member of the opposite sex. There's no limit to my love for them, but as I watched this strange mood fall over them all, I felt as if I had suddenly understood just what miserable creatures women really are. But at the same time, I couldn't stop myself from thinking that they're just so beautiful, these sisters of mine.

So, if he tried to kiss me, I might not be able to stop myself just with slapping him. No, I would kiss him back, I would give my whole body to him over and over again, I would give him more than he could possibly bear, and then I would cast him aside, just like that. I mean, wouldn't that be so fitting? And then I would say: *Sex? I'd do that with any man. I never once thought* you *were special.* Yes, if only my sisters would do that. But they're different. The three of them have really fallen for him, from the deepest depths of their hearts. Just thinking about it makes me so frustrated. It was like these New Women, born and raised in this neighborhood of mine, were about to end up getting stained by some outsider. Like they would cease to be my sisters who had hauled the *mikoshi* through the streets rather than riding docilely on top.

* * *

"Hey, Mom, what was it like having sex with Dad, before you broke up with him?" Moeko asked between sips of her Denki Bran.

Mom was drinking a glass of Denki Bran as well. She turned red and let out a laugh.

That night, my sisters and I all went with Mom to this cinema-themed jazz café, a place called Eigakan. Us sisters are all pretty big on the atmosphere here, the walls all covered with posters for films like *Hiroshima mon amour* and *Last Year at Marienbad*. Mom has always been a big fan of Alain Resnais, and when we were young, we would all watch videos of his films together. And so the five of us were practically regulars, and had been ever since I was a kid. Sitting in this jazz café, drinking Denki Bran.

"Well, your father, you know, he wrote about it, the first time we did it, in his diary, and then, one day, I stumbled across it, and he'd written all this stuff about finding the delta zone, it was so funny!"

We were all drunk, and immediately burst into laughter. Mom always talks about sex when she's drunk. And we all keep giving her one glass after another, all the while showering her with questions to get her to keep on talking.

"So, like, was it good, having sex with him?" Meiko asked.

"Well, you know, he wasn't exactly well-endowed, but his technique wasn't half bad."

She was laughing along with the rest of us, but Yōko still hadn't asked anything, so I thought that I would take a turn.

"Mom, how old would he have to be, a guy you'd want to have sex with? Younger than you?"

"Ah, a young guy would be wonderful. I wouldn't even mind if he were young enough to be my son. Yeah. A guy around your age would be nice."

At that moment, a deafening clang rang out.

"The same age as Nanako? You mean, someone like Tamura?" Moeko asked.

Right, I realized. *If it were a classmate or someone like that, he would be around Tamura's age.*

"Who's Tamura?" Meiko asked.

"One of Nanako's college friends," Yōko answered. "I've seen them walking around town together every now and then."

"What kind of friend?" Mom asked.

"He's just a friend," I said. "We aren't dating or anything."

"You know, girls, I'm fine with you all having boyfriends, but you shouldn't hang out with guys who want to take you to bed straight away, you know."

"I know," I responded flatly.

"But Mom, that kind of thinking is really old-fashioned, you know?" Meiko said. "If two people really love each other, they should be able to have sex whenever they feel like it. That's what I think."

"That's how all young people think. Believe me, I know. But you mustn't give yourselves away like that."

Moeko turned toward Meiko. "Oh? Do you have someone in mind?" She was clearly thinking about S, but Meiko said nothing in reply.

I was starting to feel embarrassed that someone might overhear us, and glanced furtively around the room. The barkeeper was standing in silence behind the counter, cooking up a Spanish omelet.

"What do *you* think, Yōko?" Moeko asked.

"I don't know," was all she said.

"By the way, they were showing *Hiroshima mon amour* at the Mad Hat," I said, trying to change the subject.

"Why?" Mom demanded. "I thought all they had was a TV? But I guess they do play videos of the Beatles every now and then . . ."

"One of the regulars really wanted to see it, so they had a screening party."

"So did they all watch it?" Meiko asked, sipping at her Denki Bran.

"Well, apart from that one guy, no one else was really bothering to pay attention. But you know that bathroom scene? Just before it started, one of the other regulars shouted out: 'They're getting it on!'"

We all broke out into laughter.

"I'll bet you whoever said that doesn't even know what it's about," Meiko chuckled.

"Obviously," I answered.

"We're probably the only people who would watch that movie together, as a family, don't you think?" Moeko asked as she cut a piece from her omelet.

"That's right, you're pretty weird, Mom," Meiko said.

"Do you think so?" Mom asked.

We were all getting pretty excited by our dirty conversation. I felt vaguely relieved that no one had mentioned S. The dirtier the conversation, the more excited us women would all get. Which is why the next time we come here, the four of us will no doubt shower Mom with yet more Denki Bran.

* * *

I was watching TV with Moeko, idling away some free time, when we decided to go to the local bathhouse. We messed around like a couple of puppies as we changed out of our clothes, playing with each other's breasts. Out of all my sisters, I like Moeko's breasts the most. Meiko is too skinny, and her breasts are meager and swarthy. Yōko's are plump and nicely pale, but their areolas are too big. Moeko, though, is slim and fair-skinned, and her breasts are close to perfect circles, like steamed meat buns.

Moeko had stripped stark naked, standing there unabashed without even covering herself with a towel.

"Nakedness is nothing to be ashamed of," Moeko said to me. "I mean, we've been coming to this bathhouse ever since we were kids, you know? We've all already seen everything there is to see."

When I thought about it, I couldn't help but agree. The counter had been occupied by a woman whom we had nicknamed Mitchan for as long as any of us could remember. She knew. Even when our bodies started changing during puberty. I can remember it so clearly. That day, my nipples had gone really hard—they had hurt so much, like someone had gone and hit them with a hammer. "It means your breasts are going to get bigger from now on," Moeko said to me. "When your nipples go hard like that, it means that your breasts are starting to swell."

"I know," I answered.

"You might end up big-chested before long, like Yōko," Moeko said, laughing.

I was overjoyed when she said that to me. I was so happy that I had brought it up with her. I wonder why I chose her to confide in, not Meiko, not Yōko, not Mom? The more I thought back on it, the more mysterious it now seemed.

That was what was going through my head, when all of a sudden Moeko called out to a young boy who had come wandering into the women's dressing room. On instinct, I covered myself with my towel. He looked like he was about ten years old and had come into the dressing room with his mother. I had instantly assumed that he had snuck inside hoping to catch a glimpse of our naked bodies, that he was old enough to be thinking about the opposite sex. And then, to my surprise, Moeko walked right up to him, without even trying to cover herself in the slightest.

"Hey. You didn't want to go into the men's bath alone, did you?" she asked confidently.

The boy didn't respond. He looked instead as if he were completely overwhelmed by Moeko's presence.

"Can't you talk?" she laughed.

The boy remained silent, averting his gaze.

"What a dull child," she said, laughing again.

How wonderful it would be if all women could be like Moeko! I wish that I could be like her. This sister of mine, who even as a kid had never seen anything wrong with people from around the neighborhood looking at her body. This sister of mine, who was so proud of her physical beauty, without ever letting herself feel even the slightest hint of shame. Me though, I can't stand this bathhouse. No sooner would I take off my clothes than my piano teacher might walk in, or a distant relative. Everyone can see me naked here, everyone can monitor my growth. And not just my body. Because when they see me, they always ask about my plans for the future. Moeko though, she's unmoved, no matter what people ask her. She might not have graduated from a prestigious university or anything, she might have already passed the usual age of marriage, but still she doesn't shy away, or try to hide anything, no matter whom she happens to bump into.

When my breasts started to swell, I felt like I was filled with sin. But Moeko wiped that stain away for me. *Just because your breasts have started getting bigger doesn't mean you've become a woman.* Those were the words that she used to wipe away my feelings of self-disgust. Maybe Moeko's different. Maybe she's never felt this way about womanhood. She's probably the only person in this whole neighborhood who can act so freely. Even though everyone here is watching on with abject curiosity, all wondering to themselves when this girl or that girl, girls who aren't their own daughters or family, will grow into women.

Moeko soon lost interest in the boy, and we went into the bath.

"Your nipples are such a beautiful color, you know," I said.

"People who have dark nipples, it's because they touch them too much, don't you think? It's all that heat from the friction," Moeko said.

I broke out into laughter. What she was saying was just so strange.

"Maybe it's a man who's been touching them," I joked.

* * *

One afternoon, Meiko came home in a really good mood, carrying a freshly cooked *taiyaki*. She set the fish-shaped cake down on the table oh-so-carefully, humming to herself as she went to boil some water.

"I'm making tea. Do you want some?" she asked.

"Yes," I answered. "Where did you get that?"

"I was walking by that place, you know, Kasenke, the one that makes the golden *taiyaki*? S was there. He gave it to me."

"Oh?" I murmured curtly.

I often went to Kasenke with Meiko, just the two of us. Out of all us sisters, Meiko is the biggest sweet-tooth. She would often buy things for me when I was a kid. She must have thought, since she liked sweet things, that everyone else must too. I wasn't particularly fond of *taiyaki*, but I was so happy whenever she would buy me one.

"Oh, I picked up this map outside the shop," Meiko said, unfolding it and passing to me. It was a literature-themed map of the Shitamachi, pointing out where this or that famous author used to live around Bunkyō Ward.

Did S take one of those maps too? That's what I wanted to ask, but I couldn't bring myself to do it. He had almost certainly taken one. After all, he had only just moved here, so of course he would want a map of the neighborhood.

My sister, my beloved Meiko. Were all her memories of going to buy *taiyaki* with me being painted over by this new one, of this one time that she had been given one from S? Was he in love with her? Was that why he had given it to her? I don't know. I just wish that he would stop, that he would stop acting like he's hinting at something else. I mean, he might have just been seeing the sights. He might have just been in a good mood, having stumbled upon a local *taiyaki* store. But my sister, my dear sister—she's in love with him, and now that he has gone and done this, she's probably going to end up thinking that he's in love with her too.

Strange visions kept racing through my mind. Of my sister, her body stuck to mine. We were being pulled apart. Why did he have to be so nice to her? It isn't like he's in love with her or anything. I'm the one who has always been in love with her. So why does he have to go and do that, like he's trying to hint at something more?

Meiko, I thought we had agreed, as a family, that none of us would ever fall in love? After Dad left, Mom and us four sisters—we had all been doing so well as a family of women. Isn't that the future that we were all looking forward to? Didn't we promise each other that we would all go to the same neighborhood old people's home?

I turned toward her. I want her so badly. I remembered us often getting into the same bed together, naked. When I told Tamura about it, he called me a pervert. *Your love for her is sexual*, he said. But he's wrong. I'm not lusting after some stranger I barely know. I mean, she's my sister. They're all my sisters. We were all one body to begin with. But then we were born, cut away from each other one by one. That's why I want him to stop, this S—to stop planting these seeds of love inside them. We don't need all that. But the visions kept racing through my head. I was teasing Meiko, sexually. Not by penetrating her with a penis or anything, but by whispering in her ear, filling her up with a poem that I had written to embarrass her. So Meiko, you don't need a man. In this community, this body just of women, any one of us can play that role. I wouldn't even mind playing it all the time. Because I don't need sexual pleasure. Because I'm not interested in that. It would be enough for me just to give you all pleasure. You see, we're all one person. So long as one of us sisters played the role of the man, it would be all self-contained. We ought to be able to do that. We're a perfect whole. Like Adam before Eve. Or like a hermaphrodite.

When I came back to my senses, I realized that Meiko had taken a bite out of that *taiyaki* as she waited for the water to boil. If I had been my usual self, I would have wanted to put that *taiyaki* that had been in her mouth between my own lips. But not now, not something that S had given her.

* * *

I went shopping one evening, to the Yanaka Ginza, when I saw Yōko and S sitting on the steps at the end of the street where you can see the sun setting over the town, smoking together. I should have just called out to her, to my beloved sister, like I normally would. But instead, and I don't really know why, the moment I saw them, I went and hid.

Yōko was petting a stray cat. I knew that she didn't have any real interest in animals. Normally, if us sisters were to go out for a walk and happened to see a dog, Yōko wouldn't want to pet it. Not at all. But S, he didn't know that. He didn't have the faintest clue. He just sat there, watching her pet that stray cat so joyfully, watching her with that content little smile of his. Did he like women who were fond of animals? I don't know. But that must have been what Yōko was thinking. She was quizzing out what made him tick.

She had decided that he was the kind of guy who likes women who dote on animals, that was why she was playing with the stray cat. Even though she didn't really like it herself. It was a calculated move. She had no taste for cats, but even so, she was willing to act as if she did in front of him. If another woman were to see her, they would probably be disgusted. But Yōko doesn't care what other women think of her, whether they're put off by what she does. She doesn't let things like that bother her. She doesn't think that there's anything wrong with her actions. For her, it was nothing more serious than petty fraud. She isn't particularly feminine, but she was willing to act feminine in front of this guy. Playing hard-to-get, pretending to be aloof. The loveliness of a peach-colored handkerchief, makeup applied so lightly that men wouldn't notice it. My sister was laying her traps, one after the next, all in an effort to make this man her own. My sister, chatting with S, sitting there smoking with him, pretending to act cool. That must be it, that's the kind of woman that he likes. Yōko had worked him out, right down to the smallest detail, and was busy now reeling him in.

I tried to ask her about it once: *How do you do it, how do you see through all these men, how do you know how to act to get them interested?* And she responded, with a completely expressionless face: *How do I get them interested? I don't know what you're talking about.*

Liar. You lied to me. You can see through them, through all these men, you know how to draw them in. I can see through you, Yōko, I can see through all my sisters, just like you can see through all these men. That's what I wanted to say. But by the look of things, no one else in my family understood her the way I do. They don't know exactly why, but they know that men like her. And they haven't realized anything deeper than that.

My other sisters have a complex about this. Especially now that S has popped up. *Why is it only Yōko who gets all the guys?* Meiko asked with a troubled look. *These men, all they ever talk about is Yōko this, Yōko that*, Moeko said bitterly. They must have both thought that all women needed to be as popular as Yōko.

I'm the only one who knows just how much effort she puts into it, into getting guys to like her. I'm the only one who can see through that seemingly carefree attitude of hers. I felt like I could do something cruel to her, holding onto her secrets like that. I could take all her secrets, bit by bit, filing them all away—and then, one day, maybe I would expose her in front of the whole family. I kept trying to imagine what would happen. But then, her reaction probably wouldn't be as straightforward as my other sisters. If I exposed Meiko's darkest secrets, she would just end up breaking down into tears. And if it were Moeko, she would see straight through what I was doing and get angry right back at me. But Yōko, if it were Yōko . . . For some reason, picturing how she would react made me feel better. She would probably feign ignorance. *You think I'm trying to get men to like me? I don't know how to do that. If there's a way, I'd love to know it.* She would probably just say something like that.

Yōko sometimes brings the topic up when we talk, always sounding like she's trying to make excuses. *Meiko and Moeko, and Mom too, they all seem to think guys like me. But it isn't true. Not one little bit.* But to me, it looked more like she was trying to conceal even that basic fact. Maybe she's realized it—that I've started catching on to what she's doing.

Oh, Yōko, I know everything. I know just how cunning you are, how difficult you can be to deal with. I know because I love you. Even if you go out in secret to meet S, even if you don't tell us sisters, I won't blame you, I won't mention it to any of the others. I'll simply love you for how thorough you are, how meticulous. I won't even try to imitate you. I just want to be enchanted by you, by your splendid worldly wisdom. Yōko, won't you show me one day, that perfect worldly wisdom of yours? And then you can take a so-what attitude, and you can say something like: *Men, you know, they really love it when you do this.* I love that kind of wickedness, Yōko. And I want you to charm S, to charm him to your heart's content. Because the wickeder you are, the greater the pleasure. It's so good I could die.

* * *

Every now and then, when it's still early in the evening, Meiko, Yōko, Mom, and I watch TV together in the living room over a plate of fruit. But not Moeko, not today—she's locked herself in her room, in total darkness. Masturbation. That's what she's doing. I put my ear up against her door. I could hear a pained voice coming from inside. It wasn't hers. It must have belonged to an actress in a pornographic video. And even though I couldn't be entirely sure, every now and then I could hear what must have been Moeko, gasping for breath. Was she imagining herself having sex with S? I could picture her in front of me, and my heart overflowed with ecstasy. It made me feel like I was doing it too.

I remember one time when she let me in on it. *You're so innocent, Nanako. Let me teach you. Women do it too, you know? I do it. There's no need to feel ashamed about it just because you're a woman. But Nanako, you have to keep it a secret from Mom and Meiko. Because they're old-fashioned when it comes to sex. And from Yōko too.*

Moeko. I'm not the innocent one. You are. That's what I muttered to myself, deep inside my heart. An embodiment of pure pleasure. That's how I think of her.

This one's good. Why don't you watch it, and try playing with yourself? Moeko said, lending me one of her videos. *I bought it at that second-hand bookstore near Dangozaka. I just walked right up to the clerk and gave it to him, like I was buying an ordinary paperback. He put it in a paper bag. I must have looked too confident, maybe that's why he reacted that way,* she laughed. *You're much better off buying them there, from that second-hand bookstore, rather than going to a video rental place. They're cheap, and maybe this is a matter of taste, but the older ones are better. The actresses are all so ugly in those old videos, don't you think? I love those ugly actresses. It makes the sex look more realistic.*

Late one night, I watched it alone in my room. Thinking about Moeko masturbating to it, a strange and sacred feeling came over me as I knelt reverently on the floor in front of the screen.

The video depicted a woman, dressed in a sailor-style school uniform even though she was obviously in her twenties, being violated by another woman wearing a leather dress. When you think about adult videos, you normally imagine a man violating a woman, so I sat there immersed in it, like I was looking at a priceless artwork. I racked my brains trying to understand why Moeko liked watching women violating other women. I mean, she isn't a lesbian or anything. And after a few minutes, it all made sense. Unlike those videos that practically

—

reach the finishing line when the man inserts his penis, in this video, the one that Moeko had given me, the actresses kept on playing with each other's breasts. The video was clearly suited for women too, what with that way that the actresses were stimulating each other's erogenous zones. And it made me so happy when I realized that Moeko's erogenous zone was probably her well-shaped breasts.

The memories came flooding back to me. Every now and then, Moeko likes to grab me from behind and hug me tightly. Her soft, warm breasts pushing against my back. It's such a gentle feeling. And the reason why she does that, the reason why she likes hugging me, another woman, so tightly from behind—it has to be because her breasts are her erogenous zone. That's what you're telling me, isn't it? I wanted to ask her. And if I did, she would probably just answer with a plain, decisive: *Yes*.

Moeko is like the clitoris in our family. She's erotic, a central, vital figure who can't be neglected or ignored. Always innocently saying such lewd things, always laughing in that loud voice of hers, always the center of the conversation. And we always find ourselves deferring to her.

* * *

"Why do you have that?" Meiko screamed.

"It's fine, isn't it? I'm just borrowing it," Moeko retorted.

"You two, cut it out!" Even Mom was starting to get angry with them both.

They were fighting over S. S again. He had given Meiko a tube of lipstick. And of course, she was busy gloating about it. *Maybe he's in love with me, don't you think?* she

106 - MAKI KASHIMADA

said. And then Moeko had gotten jealous, and had secretly used that tube of lipstick for herself.

My sister gave it to me when I went home a while back. Apparently S had said something along those lines to Meiko. *She didn't want it, but it's brand new, so she thought I might as well give it to someone else, you know?*

"What's the problem? He gave it away so it could be used!" Moeko said.

Indeed. *One of you can use it, right?* That was what he said, when he gave it to Meiko. So maybe it did belong to all of us.

"But he gave it to *me*. So it's mine."

"Only because he bumped into you at the library, right?"

Meiko was honest to a fault. All she had to do was say that he had given it to her as a present. That's probably what Yōko would have done. No—Yōko would have probably kept the whole thing to herself. But Meiko had wanted to boast about it. I'm sure of it. *When I went to the Hongō Library today, right, I bumped into S there. What a coincidence, don't you think? He was looking at the display for the novelist of the month. And when I went to say hi to him, he gave me this. Here.* That was what she said as she waved that tube of lipstick around.

When I heard that he had been hanging around the novelist of the month display, I couldn't help but think that he sounded like the kind of literary snob who goes on about how he's studying novels. But in the eyes of my sisters, his enthusiasm was something to be admired.

You or your sisters can use it, he said to me. So if you want to try it, I'll let you borrow it. But you have to ask first. That was what Meiko had said. So basically, it was never only hers, and it should have been fine for Moeko to use it too.

But Moeko has always been a sore loser, and the way that Meiko had explained it all must have really grated on her nerves. And so she had gone and used it without uttering a word to anyone.

"You thief!"

"What? It isn't yours!"

The two of them lunged toward one another.

"You two, stop it!" Mom screamed.

I glanced across the room, my interest suddenly shifting to Yōko. She was perfectly composed, busy occupying herself with the brie cheese and Earl Grey tea that Mom had bought from the Queen's Isetan department store at Koishikawa. She had remained silent the whole time, simply enjoying the food and drink.

Yōko. Maybe it was Yōko who had used the lipstick. But it looked like that possibility hadn't even occurred to Meiko. At times like this, Moeko is always the one who gets blamed first. She can be pretty tactless, and she doesn't have Yōko's innate sense of cunning, so if she were to use it without saying anything, it was obvious that she would end up getting caught out.

"Why . . . ? Why . . . ?" Moeko began to cry. "It isn't even yours! He only gave it to you because you ran into him at the library, that's all!"

But that wasn't all, was it? Moeko understood that better than anyone. *If he was going to go to the library, why didn't he bump into* me *there? Maybe he would have given* me *that tube of lipstick, and then* I *would have had an excuse to talk to him.*

That's what happened, isn't it? That's what she wanted

to ask Meiko. Moeko was so jealous, so envious, that she couldn't even understand her own feelings anymore.

That's what happened, isn't it? Isn't it, Meiko? This month's novelist is Kawabata Yasunari, right? Are you a fan of his? That's the kind of conversation you had with him, isn't it?

This had probably all occurred to Moeko only subconsciously, but she was so paranoid about Meiko and S having just such an exchange that the mere possibility of it only ended up fanning her jealousy.

Yōko, her expression perfectly composed, continued to sip at her tea, as if savoring the flavor.

* * *

Meiko, Moeko, Yōko. My three bewitching sisters. Please kill me. Mess me up. The visions kept on coming. I could see them playing with the phallus that I shouldn't have. And then, when I finally became one with them, there I was, melting away into nothingness. Maybe this is what it means to feel in love, I wondered. I had never seen anything particularly charming about S. That was why I didn't have much reason to fight with my sisters anymore after he popped up. I was on neutral ground.

But, I thought, it was without a doubt thanks to S that my sisters had become even more enthralling.

Ever since that S moved here, Meiko and Moeko have really fallen out, Mom said to me one day. *Even Yōko's holed herself up in her room ever since the two of them started fighting. What on earth has happened to those girls? I wish that man had never come here.*

But Mom, that's wrong, I murmured in my heart.

They've always been that way. Jealous, secretive, stubborn. To me, on the other hand, ever since S appeared, the three of them had become only more attractive.

Compared to my three sisters, I don't really have much drive, or a sense of self for that matter. I've always had this mental complex. I've never once understood what I want, or what's right. For example, I've never been in love. I've only ever dated guys who have asked me out first. My individuality, my sense of being, they've all been stolen away from me—my three sisters' personalities have robbed me of them all.

Is what I've been doing really so sinful? Is it wrong to want to be like silk, to want to be dyed the colors of my sisters? Hey, Mom, do women exist to be dyed the color of men? To be dyed by someone else—is that only allowed during the act of making love? I wonder whether I'm a bad daughter.

I'll be sucked dry by my sisters. They'll caress my body, my heart, until my very existence turns into nothing. When my sisters die, I'll probably end up disappearing. Not dying—disappearing. There would be no pain. It wouldn't bother me at all to just turn invisible and fade away.

People will point out at me as I make my way through the Yanaka Ginza, shopping basket dangling from my hand: *Look, there's someone who's lost themselves. Make sure you don't end up like her! You've got to be able to stand and walk on your own two legs!*

I don't know why I'm so disappointed with *love*, with *life*. They're all just so boring. I'm just completely taken by my sisters, my sisters who don't let themselves get overwhelmed by such things, who are able to go on fighting fearlessly among themselves over the same man. They're my whole standard of reference. My personality only serves to add something to theirs. It might not even add anything. I'm just an echo of them. But it's an erotic experience, this way of being.

Meiko, squeeze your hands around my neck. Moeko, stab me with a knife. Yōko, put your mouth to mine and fill me with poison. I'm getting close to them, slowly, little by little. I'm becoming one with them. Like ice melting drop by drop. My sisters are a coordinate axis, and I'm the mathematical function that draws a phallus over them.

I don't have my own story. My story is that of my sisters. They laugh, they get angry. It's composed of those kinds of things, this story of mine. I watch them all closely, like a blouse clammy with sweat. After all, the youngest sister always takes the supporting role.

My sisters might teach me how to play bad one day, like they did back when I was a kid. *Do it naturally! Your heart, your body, don't hold back, lay it all bare, there's nothing to be ashamed of. But don't tell Mom. She'd probably say it's wrong. But it isn't. It's completely natural. I mean, if we're all honest about our desires, of course we'd want to mess around like this.*

Mom would probably get angry. That I might die and go on living inside my sisters. But that's the only way that I *can* go on living. All I can do is face my beautiful sisters head on, and lose myself inside them.

* * *

The day came out of nowhere. Mom saw Yōko strolling through town hand-in-hand with S. That was pretty sloppy of her, I thought. I wondered whether the power of love had paralyzed all those qualities that defined who she was.

"Just what exactly is going on between you two?" Mom demanded.

Yōko, however, kept silent.

It wasn't like Mom was saying that she couldn't go out on dates. She had young daughters, so it was only a matter of course that they would want to hang out with guys. She of all people ought to have understood that. But this time, that person was S—and that was why she would have none of it.

Meiko and Moeko listened in as Mom kept on questioning Yōko in the living room.

Yōko remained silent for a short while, before finally opening her mouth. "I'm going out with him."

At this, Meiko burst into tears.

"You two, leave us alone for a minute!" Mom shouted.

Finally, she let out a tired sigh. "It isn't like I'm telling you not to go out with boys, you know," she said, as if reciting a line from a movie. "But out of everyone you could have chosen, why did it have to be *him*? Even since that man popped up here, you three seem to have all lost your minds. Nanako is the only one of you with any sense. Just because some strange young man's moved here, you three have all managed to convince yourselves that you've fallen in love with him. Haven't you?"

"That isn't it," Yōko said. "I'm serious about him. We've even promised to get married next year."

"Marriage? You're only twenty-one! You'll meet all kinds of men in the future! And what about finishing your education?"

"I'll quit."

Mom sighed again. "And what does he do for a living? I see him out and about all the time during the day. Don't tell me he works at a nightclub or something?"

"He's working part-time at the moment. But he's going to be a filmmaker. A director."

"A film director? Do you really think he's got what it takes for that? I'm not saying it's impossible, but you do realize that only a handful of people are ever able to achieve anything even remotely close to that, don't you?"

"He's talented. And besides, I'll work too, until he's able to make it happen."

"Don't be stupid. That means *you'll* be supporting *him*. I won't allow it."

"If I can't marry him, I'll die."

There was a loud smack. Mom had slapped her. Yōko burst into tears.

Yōko, normally so cool and dry, was shedding tears. Yōko, always so calm, who hardly ever fought with us sisters. How on earth had S managed to stir up her passions like this? Was he really that special? I couldn't understand it. I just couldn't understand what was so attractive about this man who had gone and captured my sisters' hearts. And all I could do was prick my ears and try to make out what she was saying. I wanted to see it too. Yōko's tears. They would be so beautiful. Like glittering droplets trickling down from a pillar of ice. That's what they would be, I was sure of it. But all I could do was imagine them. Yōko's tears. Welling up as if from an underground water vein. Because that was what they would be. Her tearful face would be completely different than Meiko's or Moeko's. Those two merely ended up looking disheveled when they wept, but not Yōko.

The visions started flashing through my mind. The image of a man called S, making Yōko cry. He was doing it out of spite, wasn't he? He couldn't turn his own dreams into reality, so he was taking his feelings out on her. He struck her. I felt a thrill as it occurred to me that this might have already happened, that it might still be happening. Or else in the throes of sex, he would take her in his arms. Roughly, violently, as if punishing her. And she would shed yet more tears at his cruelty. *Stop it, please! I can't stand it anymore! It's too good! No more!* That's what she would be crying out as the tears ran down her cheeks.

That was why I wanted to see them. Yōko's tears. Every drop would be like shards of glimmering crystal. Flawless. Perfect. Because what else could they possibly be? So I made that man into a terrible person, all to make Yōko cry. In my mind, I made him into someone who couldn't love anyone, into an embodiment of pure malice.

* * *

After that, Meiko and Moeko stopped fighting with each other. Indeed, there was no point fighting over S anymore. Nor did they show any sign of prejudice or ill-will toward Yōko. It was like they had both climaxed and were now overcome with exhaustion. My three sisters, and Mom, and me—the five of us went back to watching TV together, none of us fighting over anything. Each of us no doubt immersed in our own thoughts.

I asked everyone if they wanted to try some chocolate that I had bought from the convenience store nearby.

"No thank you," Meiko answered forlornly.

I tried to offer some to Moeko.

"Chocolate? Ah, okay. I'll try some. It's good for your health, after all." She took a piece into her hand, staring at it vacantly for a short while.

I turned toward Yōko. She was watching the TV so intently that she probably wouldn't respond even if I asked her, I thought. I withdrew the hand that had begun to offer her a piece.

For some reason, we were all watching TV together. I couldn't stop thinking about my sisters and Mom. Whatever it was that the people on the other side of the screen were saying hardly even entered my mind.

All of a sudden, a great sigh emanated from the TV. For some reason, that startled me, and I glanced at the screen. It looked like we had all been watching a health program.

"This disease has a long incubation period. By the time it's discovered, it's already beyond curing. Death is the only outcome."

What kind of illness could it be? I wondered. Could it really be that horrible, this disease? Maybe I should have been paying more attention.

Even Mom, usually so fastidious about health issues, was watching the program in idle silence.

"We've asked our guests to make a note of their lifestyle habits, to see whether or not they have a chance of developing it."

Insufficient sleep, smoking, alcohol, an oil-rich diet. The things that they mentioned would apply to just about anyone.

"To our viewers at home, if you're living like this, this disease may soon affect you too. In fact, it wouldn't be at all surprising if it's already struck, so be sure to see your doctor for regular checkups."

NINETY-NINE KISSES · 115

"We might end up dying too," Meiko said idly, her voice betraying her lack of concern.

"Everyone dies one day," Yōko responded. She too seemed preoccupied.

"There's no escaping it," Moeko murmured in agreement.

My sisters' words piled up in my heart like snow.

The questions echoed in my mind: What exactly is haunting us sisters? Are we all afflicted by some incurable disease too? Hey, Mom, why did you give birth to us? Why did you only have daughters, and four at that? If you had had a proper mix of boys and girls, my sisters wouldn't have ended up all getting charmed by the same man.

It's unnatural, this situation, all of us sapped and listless. It feels like a funeral. The only words that come to mind are melancholy and darkness, but it's also somehow sacred. One day, we might all be featured in a human-interest piece in the local newspaper. Four sisters, bringing themselves to ruin. Yes, this ruin would include me too. It had probably begun even before S showed up. Five women, living together almost incestuously. How are we supposed to keep on going, how are we supposed to keep on living? It's all over. Ahead of us, there's only death. I could feel it instinctively. Children will offer white flowers to our pale bodies, like it's some kind of celebration. But it'll still be the end. The children will be so innocent that they won't have realized that yet. They'll just keep giving us more and more flowers. And they'll probably say: *Those women, they're so pretty.* Yes, I know. I know just how pretty we all are.

* * *

Yōko broke down into tears. Only in front of me, though. *It's over,* she said. *It's all over. Everything that we've ever had as sisters. I'm not saying this because I loved him, you know? I mean, he's so dependent, so useless. And look what he's done to us all. He's ruined us. Please. Let me cry with you, let me cry on your lap. You understand, don't you, Nanako? You can see what's happened, can't you? All I can do now is cry. There's nothing else left.*

I startled at this, at brushing up so close to her beautiful soul. She was so different now from the person whom I had seen smoking and acting like a delinquent in front of S. Why, I wondered, why did my proud Yōko have to end up falling in love with that guy? I could hardly believe it.

None of it makes any sense. Men, women, the way they fall for each other, she said, as if she could read my thoughts. *I mean, it's not like I chose to fall in love with someone like him.*

Yōko, you really are so pure. I feel like I've known it for the longest time. You're tough, you're artful, but in a different way to most other cunning women. That man should have realized it by now too. That this place is too elegant to really call a Shitamachi. It was always his intention just to play around with an easy Shitamachi girl, wasn't it? But he must have realized his mistake by now. The real inhabitants of this neighborhood have been living here for generations. From my grandfather's, my great-grandfather's time. And we're always dumbfounded by the strangers who come here. They expect to see the spirit of the Shitamachi in each of us as well. The idea of a loose, rundown Shitamachi, whatever that's supposed to be. It's all a lie. If they could see who we really are, they would know that we're reserved, that we're shy around strangers.

So I know. I know just how much you've been overdoing it trying to meet his expectations. That you were simply playing the role of a Shitamachi woman. Meiko and Moeko may have just been watching him from a distance, that man, that stranger. But *I* know. I know that you, Yōko, you gave your whole body to him. And, for you, that was your ruin. And for Mom, it no doubt means disgrace.

But the thing is, we're all dying to know. About this person who has come here to our neighborhood. I wonder whether he has found anything around here that really conjures up the image of a Shitamachi. People call this a town of literati, but I wonder whether there's anything left of that old-fashioned spirit.

He might be drinking at the Eau de Vie right around now. Or maybe, I wondered, he'll be making his way up Sansakizaka in the middle of the night, almost all the way to the cemetery. Only an outsider would think to go there.

Please, please sleep with me tonight, begged Yōko, normally so resolute in her solitude. Dressed in a tanktop, I crept into her bed, like I used to so long ago. I was brimming with curiosity, and ended up showering her with questions about S. To the point that even I wondered whether I wasn't being rude. Where do you go on your dates? How often do you have sex? That kind of thing.

He still acts like a tourist, Yōko answered. *He's so interested in this neighborhood that he just can't help himself. He started going on about the Yasuda Kusuo Residence, right, and even suggested we go there on one of our days off. Why would you pay to go somewhere like that? No way!*

Then he started going on about the Shimazono Residence too. That there's a concert coming up there, or something.

Yōko kept on talking.

I guess we just gradually started having sex more and more. He only really treated me well the first time though. He must have thought that I'd pretty much just offer myself up to him. It's like he doesn't have a clue what people are like around here. He doesn't even understand the difference between a Shitamachi and a loose, sleazy town. He practically sees us Shitamachi women as prostitutes. Guys from around these parts are so much better.

A lot of people think of our town as the quintessential Shitamachi, but that image just leaves us feeling all flustered and confused. Because it couldn't be any further from the truth. I mean, the vast grounds of Nezu Shrine lie in the middle of a quiet residential area. Like an empty, blank space. Foreigners and tourists from all over the country make their way there, maps in hand. But us, we went there for sketching practice when we were in elementary school. There was never anything particularly special about it for us. We didn't understand the first thing about it. Now that I thought about it, Yōko's unhappiness must have started all the way back then.

* * *

After a while, Yōko and S's relationship became more or less official. Mom gave up on trying to get them to break up. S started to come to our house to pick Yōko up whenever they went out on dates. He came across as a decent enough young man, his appearance always neat and tidy. Meiko and Moeko, though, had grown afraid of him.

They thought of him now as some kind of delinquent, and did everything they could to avoid him. Whenever he came to pick Yōko up, we would always hide in our rooms and pretend that we weren't home.

At such times, Meiko's emotions would start getting the better of her, and she would come stumbling into my room. *I'm scared,* she would say. *Yōko really is going out with him, isn't she?* Her voice would be so calm as she asked me this, as if she had completely forgotten that her own feelings for him had burned so strongly. And I would reach out to hug her. *It's okay,* I would say, *there's nothing to be afraid of.* Her delicate build is so feminine. I felt like I could read her future. She would probably get married to a childhood friend of hers living somewhere just around the corner.

Meiko. So innocent. She's thirty-two years old, and still she can't do anything by herself. She can't even cook or do her own laundry. Mom's the one who washes her under-wear. But she's fine this way. That's what I've always thought, ever since I was a kid. But as for how our neigh-bors see her, none of us has any real idea. Except when it comes to the old woman living next door, that is. *That Meiko of yours is such a devoted daughter,* I overheard her say once, completely missing the mark. She seemed to think that daughters should stay with their families, and that the fact that Meiko still lived with us all was a sign of her filial dedication. But that wasn't the case at all.

Even now that Yōko was openly dating S, Meiko didn't harbor any sense of envy toward her. It would only be nat-ural to be jealous in her situation, but she had never envied anyone anything. It was as if she lacked the basic ability to feel those kinds of emotions. *I'm worried about Yōko,* was all she said. *I feel like she's drifting away from us, Nanako. I feel like I'm all alone. And I'm scared, so scared. Like something really bad is going to happen, and there's nothing I can do about it.*

Ever since she had found out about Yōko and S's relationship, Meiko had started having nightmares. She had even been prescribed a course of Halcion to help her deal with everything. And whenever she had one of those nightmares, she would come and wake me. *Hey, Nanako, I had a bad dream. S was going to kill me. I've got a really bad feeling about everything.* And I would say to her: *I'll get you some honey tea. It's okay, there's nothing to be afraid of. Yōko won't stay with him forever. Even she must know that.*

Really? Meiko would look up at me. She has an intuitive ability to see through people's lies. So I stared straight into her eyes, to prove to her that what I was saying was true.

Meiko wouldn't be able to break out of these cycles of anxiety unless she thought that I was telling her the truth. But even though I had basically just made it all up, she didn't accuse me of trying to trick her. She probably hadn't even fully realized that she herself had seen through the lie. In her anxiety, she couldn't fully bring herself to go along with what I had told her, but she had seen through it only vaguely, without fully understanding.

As I watched her, I started wondering how everything would have played out if *she* had been the one whom S had chosen. I could practically see him, this S who knew nothing about the delicate woman in front of me, rolling up her skirt and snatching her panties. If he did that, Meiko would probably suffer a complete mental breakdown. I felt a strange thrill at the cruelty of my imaginings.

Meiko is so pure that she comes across as simple-minded. She has always known the difference between truth and falsehood. She just hasn't realized that. She doesn't understand her own true nature. If someone in the family tells a lie, she gets scared. But she herself doesn't understand why she ends up feeling that way.

Her chastity was such a waste. It occurred to me that she might one day end up losing that chastity in a random act of capriciousness. And I started to feel better, imagining such things.

In fact, Meiko might even be better suited to S. Her scrawny body was perfectly proportioned for stirring a man's lust—an altogether different kind of lust than what S must have felt toward Yōko.

Sometimes, I find myself wanting to say cruel things to her. *You're the kind of person who ends up getting sold off to a foreign country, as a prostitute. That's your fate.* That's the kind of thing that I want to say. Because she really is stupid, to the point where she might actually end up believing everything that I said to her.

When would she finally realize what it means to be with a man? I wondered. I could imagine some faceless man, doing to her the kinds of things that S does to Yōko.

Like dyeing a white dove red with blood.

* * *

A little while after that, Meiko brought another *taiyaki* home. This time, though, it wasn't a treat from S.

Were those maps of the Shitamachi still there? I asked.

They're gone, Meiko answered. *They must have been put out there then because it was a holiday, so I guess I just got lucky. It looks like they're for tourists after all.*

Ah, I thought. So this town only shows its touristy face on holidays.

I could see them both, in my mind. S eating a golden *taiyaki* with Yōko. It must have been a holiday. That was why he was carrying a map of the Shitamachi. And for some reason, as I watched them, feelings of hate started welling up inside me.

Hey, Nanako, I've been thinking that maybe I've been leaning on you too much, Meiko said to me. *Whenever I end up like this, breaking down into tears, you're always the one who hands me a box of tissues. Nanako, you're such a dedicated, wonderful little sister. You're wasted on me. When all this stuff with S started getting out of hand, I was really jealous at first, you know? But it was always you who comforted me. You made me that honey tea. Not just tissues, but honey tea too. Even in the middle of the night, you'd stay by my side. But I've given up feeling jealous about Yōko. I've been thinking, if she marries him, I'll give her my blessing. And as the eldest daughter, I'll have to take the lead in preparing the wedding ceremony. She's got such nice, pale skin, not to mention her good looks. With her chest, she'd look beautiful in a low-cut dress, don't you think? I'll have to decorate it with white roses. It sounds wonderful, doesn't it?*

She might be the eldest of us sisters, but Meiko always acts as if she's the youngest. She's so delicate, so helpless, that she would probably be completely crushed if even the smallest misfortune were to befall her. What's happened to you, Meiko? What's going on in your heart? Just what kind of fancy has thrown itself on you?

Meiko, please, heal Yōko. Even a fragile person like yourself ought to be able to do that much. She's still stuck dating that guy, that man who came here as no more than a tourist. Why don't you tell her how you're feeling, Meiko? *I'm fed up with him,* you could say. *I can't take it anymore. I can't even bear to walk around town anymore, this place that's been my home since I was a kid.* You could let Yōko break down into tears and cry on your lap. Please, Meiko, you could cry along with her. You could make your face look so wretched, so much more unsightly than hers.

I was still the only one who could see through it all. I was still the only one who could see that Yōko was fed up with that guy. But I hadn't been able to bring myself to tell anyone. How even though she's fed up with him, she trembles with fear at the very thought of breaking up with him. I had no idea, none whatsoever, how to put that contradiction into words.

But Meiko just kept going on and on about how happy Yōko would be once she married him. *He'll be a great film director one day, don't you think?* That was all she talked about. *Mom says he's taking advantage of her, but there's no way that could be true. She's just investing for the future. I mean, it's unthinkable, right? This idea of Yōko supporting some useless guy. That isn't her. She's always been able to see through people, always been able to size them up, even when she was just a kid.*

Meiko just doesn't know the truth. About men and women. About sex and love. But she's fine that way. I mean, I don't really know much about them either. And I don't want to. Meiko's fine not knowing what Yōko's going through. Because love with some outsider—for Meiko, that's out of the question. I alone would violate her, in my

124 · MAKI KASHIMADA

mind. I would make her mine. Because she's a good woman, with a noble character that would be completely wasted on someone like S.

* * *

One day, Yōko invited me to go with her to Hanake, just the two of us. We ordered the jumbo *gyōza*, and even though it wasn't the season for it, some shaved ice too. They do shaved ice at Hanake all year round. *I've been keeping this place a secret from S,* Yōko told me. *I don't know why exactly, but I felt like I wanted to protect it, to at least keep this place safe, or something like that. We go to the Pomegranate whenever we come to Yanaka. After a while, I just couldn't keep going past the Dandanzaka steps at the end of the street anymore, you know?*

Our jumbo *gyōza* arrived, a plate for each of us.

They're so huge, Yōko exclaimed. *Were they always this big? I mean, we've been coming here ever since we were kids, right? So if anything, they should feel smaller, don't you think? But they just seem to keep getting bigger and bigger.*

There were five on each plate, but we ended up leaving two untouched on each of them. All of a sudden, Yōko broke out into a laugh. *It looks like we would have been fine ordering just one plate. We pretty much always end up with a full serving left, don't we?*

We left the restaurant, and made our way down the Dandanzaka steps hand in hand. Yōko's soft palm enveloped mine. It was just like I remembered, just like when I was a kid. But I couldn't help but feel as if something inside me had changed.

As I wondered what exactly it could be, I felt a strange numbness in the corner of my eye. Before I knew it, that numbness had disappeared, and in its place a tear was running down my cheek.

I hugged Yōko close. Yōko hugged me back. *You're afraid, aren't you?* she said to me. I myself didn't know whether that was the case. But Yōko is so perceptive. She could no doubt read my emotions better than I ever could.

Yōko's voice, that warm, kind voice that had realized that I was afraid, gradually became tearful. I looked up at her. I felt a sudden urge to kiss her, to push my lips up against her own. To kiss her, the way that lovers kissed. I didn't know why I wanted to do it. And I knew that I shouldn't. But I didn't understand why that was either. It should have been fine for these irrational thoughts that I had for my three sisters to come to the fore. I mean, I've felt this way for so long that they all ought to have realized it by now. One day, they'll return my feelings. That's what I should have been thinking. But as we stood there like that, as Yōko held me and I held her, for some strange reason I found myself hesitating.

And then it occurred to me. These emotions, this sense of fear, they had all arisen from the realization that I shouldn't kiss her. This time of my life when I could do anything, this age of innocence, was for me, it seemed, nearing its end.

Tears rolled down my cheeks, one after the other. If I had actually kissed my sisters, I thought, surely I would have cried even harder. But no, I knew that wasn't true. I couldn't do it. I couldn't kiss them. And now, I knew, that was precisely why I was crying so wretchedly.

I stood there for the longest time, tears running down

my face. Yōko offered me that peach-colored handkerchief of hers. It was so soft, and smelled so nice. She wasn't using it to attract men. Now, she was handing it to me, her little sister possessed with such obscene thoughts, as if to heal me. She's cunning, and men, for some reason, find her especially attractive. But looking at her now, what I saw wasn't that side of her, nor was it a woman for whom men would fall head over heels. She was just her normal self. And yet, she was able to heal me. She's so strong, I thought. If she had been an average woman, if she had ended up becoming average at the hands of some man, that charm of hers would have completely vanished. But Yōko was different.

* * *

Moeko asked me to go with her to Eigakan. I felt a strange incongruity at that. What on earth could have been going through her mind? I mean, Eigakan had always been Mom's territory.

She ordered a glass of rum, I some lemonade. Neither of us was in the mood for a Denki Bran.

"There's something that I've been wanting to show you all day. That's why I suggested we come here," Moeko said, before passing me a small photo album. It was filled with pictures of me as a baby with my three young sisters.

"When you were born, we were all so happy. But you know, Yōko was especially thrilled. She must have been so pleased to finally have a sister younger than herself. She was the one who named you. *Nanako.*"

Yōko always wanted a younger sister, someone who looked like her, Moeko said. *Us sisters, we all look alike,*

and even our names are similar. It was Yōko who first real-
ized that.

I flicked through the album. I came across a picture of
Moeko straddling Yōko. Just as Moeko had pressed her
breasts, one of her erogenous zones, against me, I found
myself imagining that, in the picture, she was rubbing
another one, her clitoris, against Yōko.

Hey, Nanako, do you think Yōko's okay? Moeko asked.
Is it really okay for her to be in love with that stranger? She
was talking about Yōko sleeping with S. It was the kind of
question that shouldn't have needed asking.

Moeko. My headstrong sister, who even as a kid, knowing that a woman's erogenous zone is her clitoris, rubbed
herself against her younger sisters. Even she was afraid of
having a physical relationship with a stranger.

No, that wasn't right, I corrected myself. It was precisely because we're sisters that she could rub her erogenous zones against us. She wouldn't be able do that with a
stranger, maybe not even with a man from around our own
neighborhood.

Moeko was saying that her mind and her body were the
same. Maybe she was trying to tell us that she loved us sisters more than she could ever love a man, just like I did.
And that she would do with us the kind of things that men
and women do with each other.

Hey, Nanako, I really do love you all, Moeko said, grasp-
ing my hand.

Moeko, unable to express her feelings of love, unsure
what to do with her body, was trying the only way she
knew how to put those feelings into words. I felt that, until
now, I had only ever seen her from behind. No matter
what happened, she had always kept moving forward. She

had never faltered. But now, I could reach out and touch that kindness of hers. And she looked back, and embraced me. I could feel the warmth of her delicate affection pressing against my skin.

Up until now, she had really just been bumbling her way through things, I thought. Even when her feelings were as benevolent as the Holy Mother's, she expressed them as if they belonged instead to Eros. But I knew it now, I could feel it. There was no woman more pure or virtuous than her.

Moeko, you should say all that to Yōko. You should tell her what you just told me. It would make her so happy. Your emotions spilling over as you let her know just how strongly you feel. She'll understand your expression of love. But no, Moeko would be too afraid, afraid that her love might be rejected. Because she wasn't like me. Until now, I've only known one way to express my feelings. If I were a man, I would want to violate you. That's what I would have said. But Moeko is different, so delicate, so pure.

One day, she'll no doubt return to her usual self. To that sister of mine who rubs her erogenous zones against us. But I won't forget. I could never forget just how immaculate her feelings are.

Moeko herself hadn't realized it. She had no idea just how pure she was. And I had no way of conveying it to her.

* * *

I went with Mom to the Queen's Isetan department store to buy something for dinner, the same as always. *Why don't we make a paella tonight?* Mom asked. So we walked through the aisles, picking out saffron, paprika, mussels, and the rest, putting them into the shopping basket one after the other.

Mom turned toward me after we finished up at the checkout. *We always end up buying so much whenever we make paella, don't we? Why don't we take a break?* she asked, and so we went to a café.

We ordered some coffee. Mom didn't say anything. There was a recording of a Brahms symphony playing in the background. The heavy sound, like a deep underground rumbling, shook my heart, but strangely it didn't leave me feeling tense or uneasy. The passions that it called to mind were healthy ones, everyday desires set to music, things like wanting to rise up in the world, or to build a successful romance.

Our drinks finally arrived. The coffee here is famously hot, and it made Mom's eyelids twitch as she took a sip.

"Hey, Nanako, about Yōko . . ." Mom, unable to stand the heat any longer, took a mouthful of water. "It sounds like she's broken up with that boy."

I sipped at my own coffee in silence. I had expected that this would happen.

"Now that she's learned things the hard way, I hope she won't get caught up with another weird guy like that."

That's not likely, I whispered in my heart. It's the weird guys who have all those weird charms. Most women end up falling for them. And Yōko is just like most women. She won't be able to stop herself from up getting caught up in the wake of another weird guy. I could already imagine it. She has just grown up a little faster than the rest of us sisters. Sooner or later, Meiko and Moeko will surely go the same way. But I wanted to ask Mom something. Even if you wind up with a weird guy, does that really leave you stained? I wanted to tell her that I had never thought of *her* that way. It seemed to me that no matter how it was abused, the human body wasn't the kind of thing that could ever be permanently tainted.

I could see them, as if right before my eyes. My sisters, each of them having found partners of their own. Even after getting married, even after having children, still fighting among themselves like children. Still frolicking about like angels. Even if the passage of time left them old and frail, even if they met with such contempt that it left not only their bodies defiled, but their spirits too, one day there they would all be, washed up against the shore, recalling the past—my three sisters, all so beautiful.

The Brahms symphony flowed over me. It sounded almost like a popular ballad, the kind of melody that always brought me to tears. I had hated this kind of song when I was a kid. But now, I felt like I could finally understand why I needed it.

* * *

Mom and us four sisters went back to sitting in the living room together, just like we used to. No one said anything about S.

Earlier that day, we had received a sample of several lipsticks in the mail. Small circles of paste on a piece of cardboard, like paints on a palette. Meiko had brought it inside and put it on the table.

She didn't wait even a moment before picking up a lip brush. Moeko was just playing around, smearing the lipstick on her lips with her finger. Yōko had her head tilted to one side, reading the text on the pasteboard under the title *Six New Shades of Autumn*. I sat watching my sisters fondly.

Mom had begun to sing "Fly Me to the Moon." It was the kind of melody that hits you like a cold, wintry wind. And then I started thinking: What was she doing? Isn't that the kind of song that a prostitute would sing? But I stopped myself. That couldn't be right. If it were a prostitute's song, she wouldn't be able to sing it in front of her four daughters. And no sooner had I realized this than my memories all began to blur together.

Six years ago, Mom had come out with an announcement. "Listen carefully, you four. Your father and I have decided to get a divorce."

Meiko immediately burst into tears. Moeko immediately went to hug her. Yōko wore a detached expression. I looked at my three sisters, completely exhausted, thinking that everything was going to descend into pandemonium all over again.

"That's fine, I guess, if it's what you've both decided. But you need to tell us why," Moeko said, her voice filled with frustration. But why on earth was she so disgruntled? It probably wasn't the fact that they were getting divorced that had upset her, but rather that news of it had made Meiko cry.

"There's no one reason," Mom said. "Is there ever really a single reason why you would break up with someone?"

Moeko was silent.

"All kinds of things happen between men and women, piling on top of one other, and people end up growing apart, you know? That's just how they are."

Hearing this, Moeko burst into tears too. Because what Mom had said was so true.

Mom had never treated us like kids. Most parents only start thinking about the budding sexuality of their children when it's already too late. But Mom was different. She had treated us like women from the very beginning. So she was breaking up with Dad the same way that any of us might break up with a boyfriend, because things had just piled up until they had become unbearable. That's what she had meant.

"Hey, Mom," Moeko said. "Did Dad give you a hard time? Did he do anything to you? If he did, tell me. I'll sue him. I'll take him to court."

"A hard time . . . ?" Mom wiped away her tears. "Of course there have been hard times. But there's been so many, I can't even remember them anymore."

A while after that, when I went into Yōko's room one day, she said to me: "Dad's got another woman. You know, apart from Mom."

I was taken aback.

"But I can't work out who's in the wrong." She was playing around with one of her desk drawers. "I'm going to see his new wife this weekend. I've already met her a few times, actually."

"How can you put up with her?"

"She's a good person. Dad said that he loved her, but that he loved Mom too. So it isn't like Mom did anything wrong. That's what he said to me." She opened the window and lit up a cigarette. "You don't like it when I smoke, do you?"

"I'm okay."

I *didn't* like it, but now wasn't the time to admit that.

"Yōko, when did you start smoking?"

"The guy I'm going out with is a smoker. I didn't like it at first either, but before I knew it, I'd picked up the habit myself." She took one more long drag from the cigarette, before crushing it out. "Hey, Nanako. You don't think very much of me, do you?"

I shook my head, taken aback by her question.

"It's okay. I understand. You don't like me, because I'm always letting these men change who I am."

"It isn't you I don't like. It's all this stuff that happens between men and women."

"I hate it too, to be honest." She lit a fresh cigarette. "You know, sometimes I get jealous of Meiko and Moeko. Like when they fight with each other. Or their idealistic view of men and all that. I'm just completely disillusioned with it all."

But you'll still keep falling in love, I thought. Yōko was made up of a lot of parts, parts that couldn't be explained through logic or reason.

My sisters all picked out their favorite colors. For Meiko, it was pink, for Moeko, brown, and for Yōko, it was a clear gloss.

Moeko and Yōko took out a pair of small brushes and began to enthusiastically apply the makeup to their lips. The three of them all jostled with one another over a small hand mirror. It was like watching them pour their burning passions into a single point, a small point of lipstick. It was like the flowers fighting among themselves at Nezu Shrine, back when S had first appeared in town. They were all staring deeply into the mirror, as if each of them was spellbound with desire for themselves.

There was nothing unusual about that. My sisters *did*

want themselves, desperately. But they knew that they would never be able to grasp what they saw in that image.

Meiko, Moeko, and Yōko scrambled over the colors, trying first one, then the next, glancing back into the mirror with each freshly applied coat. It was as if the three of them were staring into a stained-glass window filled with the faces of saints, as if they didn't really care which of them they saw staring back.

"Meiko," I called out.

"Sorry, I'm a bit busy right now," she said without even glancing my way.

"Why don't you go watch some TV?" Even Moeko wasn't paying attention to me.

When I turned to Yōko, she didn't even respond.

I approached Mom. "This is so boring!"

"Truly," she sighed. "Those three really do go crazy about their makeup," she said, sounding strangely happy about it.

The weather forecast was showing on the TV. "We can look forward to blue skies today, not a cloud in sight," the announcer said decisively. The woman's voice seemed to pierce the cloudless sky, to tear into my eardrums. The sound left me feeling like I was listening to a soprano singing an aria, to the cruel, enthusiastic cries of women.

"We're done."

Moeko appeared by my side, Meiko and Yōko tagging along behind her.

"What do you think?" she asked. She no doubt wanted to hear which of them I thought was the most beautiful.

Neither Meiko nor Yōko said anything to challenge that. They wanted to know too. All three of them wanted to hear what I thought.

"Moeko's color is a bit plain," Meiko said. "But then your sense of fashion has always been like that."

"How rude," Moeko replied angrily. "*Yours* is too gaudy. Why don't you try picking something more suitable for your age, for once?"

"Come on, you two. Stop criticizing each other all the time," Yōko said.

"You're a nasty one, Moeko. Give me back that suede miniskirt I let you have last winter."

"I thought you gave it to me. You know, seeing as it's too gaudy for you these days," Moeko responded defiantly.

"But I bought it at that secondhand store the first time I went to Paris. I've been meaning to save it, as a memento. Give it back."

"A memento? Don't be stupid. Besides, miniskirts don't suit you anymore, not at your age."

"What did you say?"

The two of them started scuffling with one another right in the middle of the living room.

Meiko had worn that miniskirt all the time when she had been a bit younger, matching it with a pair of long boots. The outfit had really suited her. But then she had decided to hand it down. And when Moeko had gotten her hands on it, she had gone looking for the exact same pair of boots too, wearing them all over the place as if trying to show her elder sister up.

I remember Yōko and Mom saying to each other that she shouldn't do that sort of thing, that it wasn't very nice to Meiko.

"This always happens with you two. That's why I don't use any of your things—not your makeup, not your clothes. I don't care how poor I am, I'll buy whatever I want myself," Yōko declared.

"Anyway," Moeko said. "Let's get Nanako to decide who's the most beautiful."

The three of them finally fell silent.

"You're all pretty, all three of you. So stop fighting." It was obvious what my answer would be, but still they insisted on asking me that mean-spirited question.

"You're such a flirt," Moeko teased.

"Really, you three," Mom sighed. "Can't you go even one day without fighting?"

"Maybe not," Yōko said. "Maybe we can't live without fighting. I mean, it's fun."

"Nanako," Moeko said, hugging me from behind, kissing my cheek. Did she leave a trace of her lipstick there? I found myself glancing down at my feet.

"Not fair, Moeko," Meiko said, kissing me on the forehead.

"Me too," Yōko added, kissing the back of my hand.

I felt suddenly embarrassed. I could hardly sit still. My cheeks were starting to burn. I wanted to run away somewhere and hide, but there was nowhere to go. That was how I felt. Why? I wondered. A feast—my three sisters and me. Even though it should have been me who had been longing for this moment for so long. Even though this should have been the realization of that sacred dream that I had thought would never come true. My sisters, on some kind of whim, had ended up carrying out this sacred ceremony. My sisters, calculating, forceful, impure, and yet also beautiful.

I wouldn't be able to withstand their malicious kisses. I was sure of it.

Moeko hugged me from behind, her arms holding me tight. "Hey, Nanako. Why don't you try putting some on as well?"

"No," I answered. "I'm not interested."

"Just a bit of gloss won't hurt, right?" Meiko said. "Hey, Yōko. Why don't you help her out?"

"Good idea," Yōko said, taking some gloss onto a brush.

Meiko and Moeko held me down. Yōko started to paint the gloss on my lips. They felt sticky. But what my sisters were doing to me was almost like the kind of sensual doctor–patient games that young kids play. My chest felt like it might explode.

"Take a look, Nanako," Moeko said, passing me the hand mirror. "See how beautiful you are?"

I looked timidly into my reflection, but there was no change.

Once the three of them had gone back to their rooms, I took another look in the hand mirror. I picked up a tissue, thinking to wipe away the gloss—but before I could raise it to my lips, I hesitated. These lips. They were Yōko's lips. And I realized then that the reason why she doesn't leave any lipstick on her cigarettes is because she only wears gloss.

I was fascinated by those lips. I touched them gently with my finger. They were moist with the gloss, and surprisingly comfortable. I would probably never forget this moment, I thought. I had learned today that I was just like Yōko. Soon, I would become a woman, like her, filled with contradiction and stubbornness.

I stared into the mirror. I looked a lot like her after all. From here on out, I would almost certainly take on the features of my other sisters too. This town, its face comprised of both glitzy Yamanote and earthy Shitamachi, was exactly the same as the pure yet dissolute faces of us sisters. And those faces, those two parts, would never be lost. Not even in the arms of some good-for-nothing man who might one day show up from somewhere far away.

About the Author

Maki Kashimada's first novel *Two* won the 1998 Bungei Prize. Since then, she has established herself as a writer of literary fiction and become known for her avant-garde style. In 2005 she received the Mishima Yukio Prize for *Love at 6,000 Degrees Celsius*, a novel set in Nagasaki and based on *Hiroshima mon amour* by Marguerite Duras, and in 2007 she took the Noma Prize for New Writers for *Picardy Third*. She was nominated three times for the Akutagawa Prize before ultimately winning the award in 2012 with *Touring the Land of the Dead*. One of her best-known works is *The Kingdom of Zero* (2009), which reworks Dostoevsky's *The Idiot* into the tale of a saintly idiot in Japan. She has been a follower of the Japanese Orthodox Church since high school.